I'VE BEEN HEARING THINGS LATELY . . .

Hearing music in my head, the unmistakable voice of Theo. *Mental fatigue, metal fatigue, battle fatigue* . . . Fiddling with a phrase, free-associating, finding the rhyme, the play on words. He never wrote a whole song until he hooked up with Carey Harrigan. She had an ear for form. He was more free-form. Not me. I can solo over chord changes, improvise, but I need a framework. I need to know the plan. And that's the thing that has me stumped. What happened was not in the plan . . .

Other Avon Flare Books by
A.C. LeMieux

THE TV GUIDANCE COUNSELOR

Avon Camelot Books

FRUIT FLIES, FISH, AND FORTUNE COOKIES

Do Angels Sing the Blues?

A.C. LeMIEUX

AN AVON FLARE BOOK

AVON BOOKS
A division of
The Hearst Corporation
1350 Avenue of the Americas
New York, New York 10019

Copyright © 1995 by A.C. LeMieux
Published by arrangement with the author
Library of Congress Catalog Card Number: 94-26411
ISBN: 0-380-72399-9
RL: 6.3

First Avon Flare Printing: August 1996

AVON FLARE TRADEMARK REG. U.S. PAT. OFF. AND IN OTHER COUNTRIES,
MARCA REGISTRADA, HECHO EN U.S.A.

Printed in the U.S.A.

RA   10 9 8 7 6 5 4 3 2 1

Dedicated
in loving memory
to my best friend Susan K. Butterworth

to
Brent C. Donahue
David M. LeMieux
David J. Morlock

and to
Stevie Ray Vaughan
with gratitude for the living legacy
of his music

SPECIAL THANKS FOR MUSIC AND INSIGHTS TO:

Eddie Beard, Andrew Gromiller, and Tom Stonaha
of Tongue 'n' Groove
Brett, Andy, Adam, Dave, and Ryan of
Antique Blues
Jimmy Vaughan
David Coe
Jimmo
Kevin Beardsworth
and
Rev. John S. Kidd, Executive Director,
Council of Churches of Greater Bridgeport
John Cottrell of Janus House
Eileen Dougherty of Fairfield High School

I'VE BEEN HEARING things lately. I'm not talking about rumors or news. Or music—hearing music in my head has always been an occupational hazard. I'm talking about auditory hallucinations—the unmistakable voice of Theodore Haley Stone.

It's 5:42 AM according to the liquid crystal display on my clock radio. The sun's about to rise and the world outside my window is still as a tomb. I'm lying on my bed watching will o' the wisps materialize, shapeless foggy bodies, like ghosts. They're hovering over the creek that winds through the salt marsh behind the dead end street where I live. Dead end.

Dead end. Hey, that's life. His voice, joking. Except that's not something he would say. Maybe I'm crazy. Or maybe I'm just tired. I've been up all night, couldn't sleep. Brains do weird things, thoughts twist like pretzels when you get too tired. Mental fatigue . . .

His voice takes it up. *Mental fatigue, metal fatigue, battle fatigue—why battle? It don't matter.* Fiddling

1

with a phrase, free associating, finding the rhyme, the play on words. Making connections. Random, though, just fooling around. He never wrote a whole song until he hooked up with Carey Harrigan. She had an ear for form, I'll admit that, maybe from being into poetry. He was more free-form. Sometimes he'd forget the words to a tune we were doing; he'd look at me and roll his eyes and grin and wing it, make up his own words. Some people can do that, play life by ear.

Not me. I mean, I can solo over chord changes, improvise, but I need a framework, at least. I need things mapped out, charted out, need to know where I'm going. I need to know the plan. And that's the thing that has me stumped: What happened was not in the plan.

There are moments that stand out like neon signs, blinking: Life Alert—Big Change. And you know at the time that as soon as you step ahead out of that moment, there's no going back.

Here's an example: the day the Stones moved into the old Captain Lemual B. Goodman House, at the end of Goodman Street, three houses down from mine. Compared to the rest of the houses in my neighborhood, the Goodman House looks like a palace. All the others are newer, thirty-or forty-year-old capes and saltboxes, colonial replicas. The Goodman House is a genuine antique. I don't think George Washington ever actually slept there, but one of his and Martha's grandkids could have, it's that old.

The place had been empty for two years. Being this historical dwelling, it had a hefty price tag for starters. On top of that, it was rundown. I'd heard my parents discuss how the new owner would have to have some serious bucks to take on the restoration. Neighborhood buzz was some ace bone doctor, with a big family to fill up all the bedrooms, had bought it.

That day, I was sitting on my front porch watching the movers cart stuff in from the truck, and deliberately not watching a game of street soccer going on in front of my house, a game from which I was excluded by virtue of my lack of coordination and speed, and my excess poundage. One of those deals where both sides made it clear they'd rather have Quasimodo with both hands tied behind his hump on their team than "The Hulk," which was what they called me then. Even my sister Allison, who's three years younger than me, and the inheritor of all the athletic DNA in our family gene pool, was playing. It killed me, but you learn to hide it.

Anyhow, I was watching the movers, thinking what a long summer it was gonna be, when suddenly a skinny, gangly kid who looked about my age, ten at the time, barreled out the front door of the Goodman House and whizzed up the street. He had a big head with a mop of curly, wheat-colored hair. Tearing after him, yipping up a storm, was a funny little dog, a mongrel with some dachshund somewhere in its family tree. It was pumping its little legs double-time to keep up with the kid.

On the sidewalk, halfway between me and the game, the kid stopped. The mutt skidded to a halt beside him. The kid looked back and forth from me to the other kids a few times. After about thirty seconds, he fixed these round blue eyes on me and nodded, like some kind of decision switch had tripped in his brain. He turned his back on the game and bolted across the lawn toward me. The dog came too.

"Hey," he said. "I'm Tee-Oh."

"You're what?" I said.

"Not what, who. My name. Tee-Oh, but you spell it T-H-E-O, for Theodore. Theodore Haley Stone." He jerked a thumb at the dog. "This is Hum. Short for Hummel, like the hotdog. You know Hummel's hotdogs?"

I shook my head.

"Oh." He shrugged. "Well, he can hum too. Listen." He broke into a chorus of "Old MacDonald." When he got to the EE-I-EE-I-O, the dog joined right in. I cracked up.

"Pretty good, huh?" He seemed pleased that I appreciated the talents of his dog.

"Yeah. He's a real humdinger." I laughed again.

"A humdinger—that's good!" Theo was nodding and grinning a cockeyed grin. "So, come on."

"Where? Why?"

"I've got this idea. I can't do it by myself. Hey, you know what time high tide is?"

I knew without even looking the tide was coming in; living by the water, you kind of absorb the tide table by osmosis, like an internal clock.

"About two hours."

"We gotta hurry then. Come on." He didn't even know my name yet, but he was like a race car, engine gunning at the line, waiting while I made up my mind. Something about him gave me a jump start. I got up and went with him. And his dog. I didn't know what he wanted to do, but I knew something—I wasn't the neighborhood outcast anymore. I had a friend.

Another neon sign moment: the first time I heard the blues.

Here's the set-up: Beginning of seventh grade, I got my first guitar, a thin, red, hollow-body acoustic electric with F-holes, an old Gibson ES-355. The kind of guitar B. B. King plays, I found out later. My father bought it off the widow of a musician buddy of his. My father's an electrician by day, a sax player by night and on weekends. He has a band, the Ron Buglioni Quintet that he's played with forever, except for a new guitarist who took over for the one who died. They have a standing jazz gig, Friday and Saturday nights at Larry's Clam House in Eastfield, the next town over from Yardley, where I live.

Now when I first got this guitar, I was like a chimpanzee with a computer; everything I did with my fingers was random. Over the course of a couple of months, I managed to pick out a few things, "Jingle Bells," "Twinkle, Twinkle, Little Star," tunes from some TV commercials, a few stray riffs from rock songs. Mostly I just fooled around. Theo and I would put on the radio, and he'd sing if he knew the words, or lip-sync, and I'd hand-sync, faking it. When Hum was around, he did background howls. Theo and I talked about how it would be cool to be in a band, but nothing happened. There was something I didn't get yet. . . .

I mean, I had the guitar. I liked music. I wanted to play. I thought that should be enough to turn me into a guitar player. My old man laughed at that.

"Hey, James, you have to pay your dues like everyone else," he told me.

"What dues?" I was ticked off. Pop had just bought me a small amplifier and I'd spent two whole hours attacking the guitar that morning, and I still stunk.

"You ever hear the story about the man and the mule?" Pop asked.

"Uh-uh," I grunted, sucking on my fingertips, which were red, dented from fretting the steel strings, and sore as hell.

"A man harnessed a mule. The mule started to walk, but the man held him back, made him wait. He said, 'Patience, mule, patience. Patience, mule patience. Patience, mule, patience. Pa—' "

"What's the punchline, Pop?" I cut in.

"Patience, mule, patience!" He grinned and socked me lightly on the arm. "Ready for some lessons?"

So I signed up for lessons and started to get the basics down. Scales, chords, the alphabet of music. I got to work paying my dues, which is just another way of saying putting in the time and effort, however much it takes, to get the results you're looking for. And I improved, no doubt about it. But all the while, I felt like I was pushing from behind, never catching up to where I wanted to be. Not that I had a clue where that was, I just knew I wasn't there.

One day, Theo called on the phone. It was August, right before school started, and we were both headed for Yardley High. It had been a weird summer for me. All summer long, I'd had this feeling like an appetite for something, but not anything edible. Something I couldn't identify that I needed to fill me up. I'd grown five inches that year, shot up to six feet, a frame on which 190 pounds sat a lot better, so I wasn't The

Hulk anymore. I wasn't sure who I was.

So Theo called. "Hey. Come on over, quick. Bring your guitar." There was voltage in his voice. I went.

I walked in the back door without knocking, standard operating procedure at the Stones'. The kitchen looked like it had been hit by a highly creative hurricane: a sink full of cut flowers from the garden, waiting to be arranged, a counter cluttered with ingredients for whatever was cooking in the big pot on top of the stove, an open book on top of a pile of mail on the desk by the phone, a basket of half-folded laundry near the door to the basement.

I could see Theo's mother in the breakfast room off the kitchen, and went over to say hi. She was sitting at the table with half a dozen postcards spread out, all stamped and addressed to Theo's older brother Eric, who'd left the day before to spend his junior year at the London School of Economics.

"Eric homesick already?" I asked.

Mrs. Stone looked up from the one she was writing and smiled. "I hope not. Just a little mother's preventative maintenance."

"Theo upstairs?"

She nodded. "Go on up. Make some noise. Please. This house always seems so huge and empty when the kids go back to school. Next year, Ellen, and after that my baby Theo. It doesn't seem possible." She smiled again, but this time with a sigh.

I lugged my guitar up the back stairway to the third floor, went down the hall, and stood in the doorway of Theo's bedroom. Theo's room was small and boxy, with a low ceiling. Bunk beds took up most of one wall, and the opposite one was plastered with black-

and-white posters of old comedy movies and shows: Laurel and Hardy, Marx Brothers, Three Stooges, guys like that. There were two dormer windows, little alcoves; one had his desk in it, and the other had a small table with the cheesy stereo he'd bought two years before, with money saved from shagging golf balls at the driving range all summer. With all the money the Stones have, you wouldn't know it from the way they dole it out to the kids.

The whole middle of the room was crowded that day with a really nice sound system, massive speakers, a CD player, a tape deck, a combination amp and tuner. And five blue plastic milk crates, filled with CDs and cassette tapes, a lot of them homemade and hand-labeled. Hum was asleep on the bottom bunk. Theo was near the desk, plugged in, headphones on, eyes closed. Whatever he was listening to was running through his body like a current.

I put my guitar case down, went over, and knocked lightly on his head. He opened his eyes and ripped the headphones off.

"You gotta listen to this." He shoved the headphones into my hands.

"Where'd you get this stuff?" I asked.

"It's Eric's. His whole blues collection. I've got it all till June." Theo was rooting around in one of the milk crates. He pulled out a tape, popped open the tape deck, and switched cassettes.

"Listen to this one. Freddie King. It'll blow you away." He stepped back and jammed the headphones over my ears.

He was right. It was like the essence had been extracted from all the songs I liked best, and there it was, straight, pure, and simple: the blues. They poured into my head, streamed directly into my blood. Freddie King, wailing and growling, crooning and moaning. But what really got me was the guitar. It was so smooth, so fluid, I felt like I was drinking the music. And it was satisfying that appetite.

From that moment on, I wasn't behind, pushing to get ahead anymore; I was being pulled forward by this determination that I was going to learn to play like that, no matter what.

We dumped the headphones, connected the speakers, and pumped them up so loud the walls were pounding with the bass. We filled that empty old house up with the blues. I got out my guitar and started hunting for the notes to play along. We played this one song over and over. By the third time around, Theo had the words down. He belted out the chorus:

> They call me the Boogie Man
> Nobody can do it like I can
> They call me the Boogie Man
> I'm a king-sized Boogie Man.

"That's gonna be you—Buglioni, the Boogie Man." Theo was boogying around the room. "Boogie Man—they'll all be saying it while you're playing it—nobody can do it like you can."

Hum had woken up when we cranked up the volume and every so often he'd go into a howling fit with Freddie King.

"Look, he's a blues hound." Theo was laughing, then he turned serious. "This is something. I can feel it. You too?"

We looked at each other and we knew. It was something.

So I became James "Boogie Man" Buglioni, a.k.a. Boog. I started by trying to learn every lick on the copies of the Freddie King tapes Theo made for me, picking out the notes, one by one, until I had it down pretty solid, the punchy runs, the bent notes. It took me the better part of two years.

Meanwhile, Theo and I put a band together. Me on lead guitar, Peter McGrath on rhythm guitar, Keith Finklestein on drums, Danny Hoha on bass, and Theo as lead singer. All through freshman year, we worked on developing a repertoire. Pure blues was my personal preference, but most of those tunes weren't familiar to our target audience, and we wanted to get hired. So we concentrated on bluesy classic rock, and stuff by guys who had covered some of the old blues songs, like Clapton, Johnny Winter, Allman Brothers, some early Stones, ZZ Top, some Hendrix. We played a lot at kids' parties for free, to get the experience.

In June of freshman year, we booked our first paid gig, Keith's sister's best friend's eighth-grade graduation party, down at the Yardley Beach Club.

"Her mother wants to know how to make out the check," Keith said. "She asked if the band had a name." We were practicing in my garage as usual, the Sunday before the party. At that point, we didn't have one. It was "Theo's band" or "Danny's band" or "Boog's band," depending on whose friend was talking.

"A name," Theo said. "Yeah. We need a name

that says who we are. Something with blues in it.''
He perched on the arm of the old brown couch we
had out there, and sat, like Rodin's thinker, one hand
holding his chin. Every few seconds he'd stick his
fingers in his hair, which was on the wild side since
he'd let it grow shoulder length. He'd stir it up like
he was trying to stimulate his brain.

The rest of us tossed out suggestions.

''Blues Express.''

''Taken.''

''Blues Machine.''

''Sounds too mechanical, too stiff.''

''Blues Boys.''

''Nah, too much like that painting of the kid in the
satin suit.''

Theo shot them down as fast as we came up with
them. Danny started noodling on his bass, the tune for
a goofy old song called ''The Name Game.''

''How about Blues Power?''

''That's a Clapton tune. The name's gotta be ours.
It's gotta be right.'' Theo was up and pacing. He
stopped and snapped his fingers. ''Where's a dictionary?''

''Den. Shelf over the computer,'' I told him.

He raced out through the door to the kitchen via
the breezeway and was back a minute later with our
big red dictionary.

''Okay,'' he said. ''Try this: Blues Thing.''

He waited.

''Blues Thing? I don't know, Theo. It doesn't seem
real specific.'' Keith is a precise kind of guy, part of
what makes him a good drummer. ''What does it
say?''

"It says it all." Theo sounded completely confident, par for the course. "Listen. 'Thing: whatever can be perceived, known, or thought to have a separate existence. Thing: an entity. Thing: the *real* substance of that which is indicated as distinguished from its appearances.' "

Our ears were definitely open. He went into a little chant. "The real thing—no big thing—wild thing, good thing, sweet thing—it's your thing." He gave the last phrase an Isley Brothers twist. Danny popped out the bass line.

"So. Whadaya think? Blues Thing."

"It has a ring to it," I admitted.

The other guys were beginning to nod. Theo gave it one last push.

" 'Thing: an activity uniquely suitable and satisfying to one.' Thing. It's a great word. Blues Thing. It's us."

So, Blues Thing was born. We started getting hired a lot, parties, not free anymore, dances at schools, and junior functions at private clubs. Summer after sophomore year, the Yardley Beach Club sponsored a "Jam-boree"—five high school bands each playing a twenty-minute set, winner chosen by crowd applause. Blues Thing won hands down. The prize was a gift certificate for five hundred bumper stickers printed with your band's name. Good publicity, and it was kind of a kick, pulling up behind a car at a red light and seeing it, white on blue, in funky letters, BLUES THING. So, we developed kind of a reputation after a while. A decent one, not to brag.

Best friends doesn't really begin to describe Theo's

and my relationship, once we got seriously into music together. It's a connection like no other, like body-surfing in this sea of sound waves you're cogenerating—feeling it as much as hearing it. Theo would belt out a line, stretch out the last syllable, and I'd be waiting to jump in with a wordless echo on guitar. Call and response, the root of the blues.

Theo was a natural, by the way, an unbelievable singer. When he opened his mouth, he mesmerized people, singing with his whole body, putting out energy that was pure Theo. He didn't need to play an instrument. He *was* the instrument.

The sun is sliding up into a barely blue sky. "Barely Blues." Could be a catchy song title. Theo's not around to write the song. Neither is Carey Harrigan. And I sure as hell won't be writing it. I haven't touched my guitar in over four months. Use it or lose it, Pop always says about music, about practicing. I've lost it.

Theo's voice again. *You gotta do it, Boog. You'll never lay it all to rest until you do.*

Do what? Forgive Carey Harrigan? None of what happened would have happened if she'd never come into the picture. I've spent the whole summer here in my room, hating her. Hate seems to have some toxic by-products, though. It feels like a poison inside me. What's the antidote?

The rising sun is lighting up the will o' the wisps now, and a light easterly breeze is nudging them along the creek, out toward the Sound. I watch and my eyes can't quite grasp the illuminated forms, because they keep shifting. It looks like a parade of angels, oblivious to this world, oblivious to me.

I've been up all night, listening, waiting. For what, I don't know, a sign, maybe. Doesn't have to be neon, just clear enough to point me in some direction.

Now Theo's singing in my head, a crazy twelve-bar blues, mixed up with church stuff. He sang in the church choir until his voice changed, and he loved gospel music. Same source, gospel and blues.

> *Well you can talk with tongues of angels*
> *   But that ain't all of it.*
> *I say you can talk like a silver-tongued devil*
> *   But what will you pro-fit?*
> *If you can't love, don't love, won't love,*
> *   You ain't worth a bucket of spit.*

I can't ignore it. It's like a call that won't stop until I come up with the right response.

2

THE FIRST TIME I ever saw Carey Harrigan was first day of senior year at Yardley High, in Miss Brockmeyer's Twentieth Century World Studies class. You couldn't not notice her when she walked into the room.

For starters, she was dressed like a walking tag sale. From the bottom up: clunky brown work boots, argyle socks, a long flowery skirt that looked like she'd mugged an old lady's bedroom window for the curtains, purple T-shirt, khaki army jacket, and a black velvet hat, the kind that looks like a squashed bell, with some droopy fake roses on the brim. Her face was pale, and she looked taller than she really was because she was so thin. Her hair, sticking out from under the hat, was fluffy and flyaway, like the tops of the reeds in the salt marsh.

She breezed through the open door, spun around, sat in one of the front seats, and plunked a worn leather knapsack on the floor. Then she picked it up again, stood, and moved to another seat, this time way in the back. By now everyone in the class, Theo and myself included, was watching and waiting to see what she'd do next. Apparently the back seat wasn't working for her either. She stood again, planted one hand on her hip, frowning, and slowly surveyed the room.

I saw her do an eye-link with Theo. I was in the fourth seat in the window row and he was sitting in front of me, next to an empty desk. He pointed to it and winked at her. Her eyes lit up, and she started over. As she approached the seat, she tripped on some air and almost took a header, but Theo sprang up like a rubber-band man and caught her in midfall. They straightened up, but didn't let go of each other.

"Well," Carey said. "See? You have to be in the right place at the right time, or the right thing won't happen."

"This is very true," Theo said.

They stood gazing at each other like long-lost twins who'd been separated at birth. Both skinny, the same blond-brown hair and blue eyes; Theo was wearing his standard ragged blue jeans and an old orange Hawaiian shirt with all the buttons missing over a T-shirt that said, "Lead me not into temptation, I can find it myself."

So there they were, Prince Crooked-Grin Charming and Cinderella before a fairy godmother spruced up her act, when Brockmeyer came in.

Miss Brockmeyer looks like a miniature fashion model, but acts like a drill sergeant. Besides Twentieth Century, she teaches World History, Government, and Economics, and she coaches girls' track. She's only five-two, but she's got a tongue like a meat cleaver, and even the wisest wiseasses don't mess with her.

"Kindly refrain from engaging in body locks in my classroom," she snapped as she took in the sight.

"Oh, yes sir," Carey said in a mock-meek lilt.

I, along with the rest of the class, held my breath. Theo and Carey slid into their seats. Carey folded her hands on her desk, model-pupil style. Brockmeyer's eyes sharpened like tiny guillotine blades and blinked her summary judgment: Cut this twit down to size.

"Keep the seats you're in now for the rest of the year unless I tell you otherwise. I'll pass around a seating plan. Fill in your names, last name first, then first name and middle initial. No nicknames."

While the seating plan made the rounds up and down the aisles, Brockmeyer handed out textbooks and gave us a syllabus for the year, which caused a collective groan—mandatory reading of *Time* magazine, weekly current events quizzes, major tests after every chapter, plus exams and two ten-page term papers.

She walked back and forth across the front of the room, her tiny high heels clicking in perfect 4/4 time, talking while she walked.

"You live in this world along with more than five billion other people. It is a small planet. The human race's track record for peaceful cohabitation is not good. In this course, we'll examine conflict, its causes and factors: economic, ethnic and cultural, political, religious. We'll look at some ongoing conflicts, examine their historical contexts. Hopefully, each of you will leave this course with a raised consciousness, so you, as citizens of the world, can improve the prospects for the human race."

She went behind her big gray desk and sat. Total silence reigned.

"So. What can you as individuals do?"

No one said anything because it seemed like a rhetorical question. Apparently not.

"Ideas. Come on."

A few tentative answers were offered.

"Join the Peace Corps."

"Recycle so there's more resources to go around."

"Go into politics and change things."

At one point, Brockmeyer looked directly at Carey and pointed her finger.

"What can *you* do to make the world a better place?"

Carey's reaction was curious.

"Me, personally?" she asked.

"Yes, you, personally." Brockmeyer mimicked her inflection.

Carey chuckled softly and looked down at her desk. "Oh, I don't know," she said. "Probably the best thing I could do to make this world a better place would be to hop on a spaceship and move to another planet."

A few snickers escaped. Brockmeyer looked momentarily stymied. But Theo had that same look on his face he'd had the first time he saw me—like he'd spotted someone outside the lifeboat, and was mentally winding up to toss them a rope and haul them in.

The last kid in the last row held up the filled-out seating plan. Brockmeyer beckoned with her hand and he brought it up to her. She scanned it, frowned, and looked directly at Carey.

"You. Harrigan, comma, Carey, question mark. What is this? Do you know your name or not?"

Carey played with a thread on the cuff of her jacket, then met Brockmeyer's stare with a little smile.

"Is there a problem?"

"Is Carey a nickname?"

It was an interesting moment, like watching the first Hatfield square off with the first McCoy, the birth of a feud you suspected would never be resolved.

"Carey is my father's mother's maiden name. Harrigan, just like the song: 'H-A-double R-I-' "

"The question mark," Brockmeyer said curtly.

Carey went on talking as if she hadn't been interrupted. " 'G-A-N spells Harrigan.' So I have two last names. And no middle name at all. People should have middle names, don't you think? The question mark is a placeholder until I decide on one. I'm open to suggestions."

That kind of approach with Brockmeyer constitutes either incredible naïveté or a death wish. They stared at each other for a long moment. Finally Brockmeyer cracked a tight-lipped smile.

"Zero is a placeholder. How about zero?"

She ignored Carey totally for the rest of the class. But Theo didn't. Every time I glanced at him, he was looking at her.

Yardley High is one of the biggest high schools in the county. There's the old building, used for administration, mostly, and a huge newer complex, built about twenty years ago. The new part is brick, modern and blocky, with four main buildings set up around a courtyard, each one called a "house," with its own headmaster: Perry House, Winston House, Matthews, and Ellis. They're all named after various founding fathers of the community, the guys who came over to New England in the seventeenth century and got the decimation of the Native American population rolling.

It seems like a lot of the time, the so-called march of civilization has been a slog through the spilled blood of other civilizations. That's how we ended up with the blues as part of America's musical heritage. Blues developed out of music brought from Africa when those founding fathers kidnapped and enslaved a whole race of people.

At one point, I went through this guilt thing, asking myself what right a white boy from the suburbs had to play the blues. It seemed like I was stealing or at least exploiting something I had no right to. Theo had a different take on it.

"We're not stealing the music. We love it. Hey, it's music, by people. When is everyone gonna get it, we're all people? Music is, like, the best common ground we have. Hey, what if Stevie Ray Vaughan had thought like that?"

Anyhow, at lunchtime and during study halls at Yardley, it's a junior/senior privilege to hang out in the courtyard. That first day, Theo and I snagged some lunch from the cafeteria and took it outside. We were sitting on one of the concrete, almost vandal-proof benches that are set around the courtyard's perimeter, chomping on chili dogs and chips. I was keeping a sharp eye out for Sharon, the former love of my life, who'd stuck it to me good and deep the previous July.

I thought the wound had scabbed over and might be healing, but I hadn't seen her since the breakup, and you never know.

Funny about being in a band. It attracts some people like a gravitational force—they want to enter into orbit around you. Not that I drew the crowd that Theo did, but Blues Thing had definitely improved my social life. Sharon, for example, pursued me with flattering persistence until she caught me. Hard to believe I'd fall for schmaltzy lines like, "You're so cuddly, just like a teddy bear," and "Your eyes look like root-beer lollipops." I swear, love can really warp your perspective. It hooked me but good.

After a while, though, I realized it wasn't me she was attracted to, it was the musician image. Now, this is a paradox. Sharon loved being a girlfriend of the Blues Thing guitarist. But behind the scenes, she started complaining how my music was more important to me than she was. After a while, I realized it was true, and one night when I didn't contradict her, she dumped me. Viciously. In public.

Since then, I'd kind of been in rehab from women. Romance, love, seemed like a net loss to me. My guitar never complained when I left it in the case. It was always there when I wanted it. And it never bitched at me because I didn't tell it I loved it. I thought I could hack celibacy for awhile.

I scanned the courtyard, didn't see Sharon to my relief, but spotted Carey Harrigan. She was sitting alone on a bench, hunched over a notebook, scribbling away, which kind of surprised me. I hadn't gotten the impression in history class that she was the overly fastidious student type who'd spend lunchtime doing homework.

"Hey, guys!" I didn't even have to turn around to know who it was: a close friend of Sharon's, ambushing us from the rear, Natalie Stewart. Natalie's pretty much queen bee of the Yardley social hive. Her folks are rolling in dough; her father's supposedly one of the top plastic surgeons in the state. Natalie looks like she stepped off the cover of a fashion magazine and never quite made it into three dimensions—something about her seems flat, packaged. She's got auburn hair and gray eyes, kind of a gunmetal color. Beautiful, I guess, and nice enough, as long as things were going her way. I'd seen her get unpleasant when they didn't.

She skirted our bench and parked herself next to Theo.

"Theo, I've been looking all over for you. You never called me back last week."

"Sorry, Natalie. Slipped my mind." He smiled, and Natalie obviously had no problem forgiving him. All junior year, she'd worked on him, and I think he took her out twice. Theo dated a lot of girls, but never seriously, never steadily. It was almost like he felt an obligation to spread himself around. I suspected Natalie was winding up for another campaign to get an exclusive on him.

"It's about the Harvest Dance. We want Blues Thing to play. Will you?" She was practically purring.

"You have to check with Boog, Natalie. He's our business manager."

She had one arm draped around his neck at that

point. Theo dropped his napkin, leaned down to retrieve it, and casually ducked outside her clutches on the way back up.

Natalie turned to me. "Well, can you? Will you?" An iota of charm had drained from her voice.

"How much?" I asked. I already knew I'd say yes, because the Harvest Dance is the big kickoff of the year. We didn't have anything else booked that night; I'd kind of been saving the date.

"Three hundred dollars," she said.

"Six hundred," I countered.

"No way—" she started to say, but I cut her off.

"Look, Natalie, you'll probably sell four hundred tickets at three dollars a pop. That's twelve hundred bucks."

"What if we don't sell that many this year?"

"What if you sell more?"

Her eyes narrowed. "How about four hundred? Come on, this is a fund-raiser for the senior trip. Where's your damn school spirit?"

Theo grinned at me from behind her and stood up. "Excuse me," he said, and made his escape.

"Final offer, half the door, with a guarantee of five hundred dollars. You know Blues Thing will pull in the crowd," I said.

She glared at me.

"You know, Sharon was right. You look like a teddy bear, but you are ice cold."

I took the fact that the secondhand insult didn't knot my gut as a good sign, and shrugged it off.

"Business is business, Natalie."

"Fine. I'll get you the contracts on Monday." She stood and tossed her hair back. Her eyes did a sweep of the courtyard, and her gaze went ballistic when she spotted Theo and realized he was with another woman. Carey Harrigan.

Even in a crowded courtyard, Carey had a knack for attracting attention. She'd put down the notebook and was sitting cross-legged on the bench, a hand resting on each knee, palms up, like she was waiting for jewels to rain out of the sky.

"Who's that?" Natalie asked. If she had fur, it would have been bristling. "I haven't seen her around before. I'm sure I would have noticed a getup like that."

"Her name is Carey Question Mark Harrigan." I swigged the last of my milk, stood up, and crumpled the carton. "She's in Theo's and my history section. Already high on Brockmeyer's blacklist."

"She looks like she was high on something when she got dressed this morning. And what's with Theo? Is he the official Welcome Wagon or something?"

I was a little surprised at the venom in her tone, and wondered if maybe behind the woman-of-the-world pose, there might not be a seriously smitten female, which to me signals danger zone. I didn't want to get drawn into it. So I flipped her an abbreviated wave and worked my way through the traffic until I was close enough to hear what Theo and Carey were saying.

"So what's *your* middle name?" Carey asked, smiling up at Theo. She was still in the Buddha pose.

"Haley," he told her.

She tilted her head. "Haley like the comet?"

"Only on my good days," he said, cracking a grin.

"Family name?"

Theo nodded. "Actually, in old Norse, it means hero." He flexed his arm.

Carey reached up and tested his bicep. "Hero?" Her voice was teasing, but not mean. "Like, 'Here I come to save the day'?" She sang the cartoon theme song.

"Could be." Theo grinned. "Need saving?"

"Could be." The smile dropped off Carey's face.

I swear, if a girl was looking at me as intensely, as needfully as that, I'd go into reverse overdrive and back off a mile or ten. Theo didn't even flinch. He caught sight of me, and motioned for me to join them. I stepped over, and he made a formal introduction.

I gave Carey a noncommittal nod, glancing down at the notebook on the bench beside her. It was one of those marble-patterned composition books. In the space for SUBJECT, were the words, *Through a Glass Darkly—The Life of Carey? Harrigan Vol. VII*, written in turquoise ink, in spidery back-slanted script. She saw me looking at it, picked it up casually, and stuffed it in her knapsack.

"We were just talking about heroes," she said.

"So tell me, who are your heroes?" Theo asked her.

"Well, Mighty Mouse really is one of them. He was the first guy I ever had a crush on."

"A crush on a cartoon character?" I snorted. "Not much future in that relationship." Something was surfacing in my reaction to Carey that really surprised me; that kind of remark isn't normally my style. A frown flickered over Theo's face, like he wondered what was eating me, but Carey looked at me curiously.

"An idea," she said softly. "You can be in love with an idea. *If* you have the imagination."

Touché. I tried to sound a little more friendly.

"Who's got the number two slot?"

She put her hand up to her chin, thought a moment, then zinged one out of left field.

"Harpo Marx."

"You like the Marx Brothers?" Theo was tickled. "See, Boog, I knew it. We're talking some serious karma here." He and Carey exchanged a look that struck me as exceedingly intimate considering the length of their acquaintance. I cleared my throat and their eyeballs broke the hold and went to separate corners.

"Why Harpo?" I asked. I was getting mildly intrigued, in spite of myself.

"Well, he's very kind. You can tell by the way he treats animals in the movies."

So she admired heroic spirit and kindness to animals. Theo could fit that bill.

"Plus he makes that beautiful music."

Music. Three for three.

"I always wanted to play the harp," Carey went on. "It seems like the one instrument in the world that's not capable of making an evil sound."

"So why don't you learn?" Theo asked.

"I don't know. It looks really hard to do. I guess I'd rather dream about doing it than try and find out I couldn't." A little smile played around the corners of her mouth, and she kind of shrugged at us, almost as if she was apologizing for something about herself.

I didn't know what to say to that.

"So how about you, Boog? Got any heroes?" Carey peered up at me from under the brim of her hat.

I didn't even have to think about that one. "The three Kings."

"The Magi?" Carey's nose twitched like she found it amusing. "You don't strike me as the religious type somehow."

I laughed. "I'm not. The three Kings: Albert, B. B., and Freddie."

"Blues guitar players," Theo told her. "Boog's lead guitarist in our band—Blues Thing. Ever hear of us?"

Before Carey could answer, Natalie sidled up next to Theo and hooked an arm through his.

"You ran away," she said, pretending to be mad.

Theo gave her the official Theo Stone never-offend-a-soul smile, then extracted her arm from his as unconsciously as picking lint off a sleeve.

"Hey, Natalie. Meet Carey. She's a transfer student."

"Really." Natalie smiled a phony smile. "So, where'd you go to school before?"

Carey didn't answer immediately. She seemed to be nervously sizing Natalie up.

"Boarding school. Brazil. My father and I have been living in Brazil for a few years."

I saw Natalie's attitude back up a few paces, as if there might be some social possibilities she hadn't picked up on, and it might not be prudent to write Carey off completely.

"So where do you live now?" Natalie continued the probe.

Carey seemed to shrink a little, and I sensed this

wasn't the start of a beautiful friendship. "Yardley Hills. Up on North Road," she said.

At that, Natalie looked like she might choke on her tongue. North Road, Yardley Hills, is one of the tonier addresses in town. A winding three-mile stretch of rolling hills, houses on lots with double-digit acreage. The Stewarts lived off North Road.

Just then Theo sat down and put an arm around Carey's shoulders, etching Carey's name in stone, as it were, on another blacklist.

"So Natalie, if you need help with the dance, decorations or anything, it might be a good way for Carey to meet—"

"No thanks. Committee's full," Natalie said.

I shook my head. For someone with such broad experience with the female gender, Theo was really missing the undercurrents.

And that was the first time I ever saw Carey do her distancing thing. Her mouth stayed smiling, but you could see something in her eyes retreat, run for cover, like in her mind she was backing down a long hallway and when she got to the end, she ducked behind a door, closed it, and was gone.

"So whadaya think?" Theo asked that afternoon. We were up at the Glacier Ice Company warehouse, stocking the truck for delivery.

The earnings from a high school band don't exactly vault you into the world of high finance. When we'd started bringing in some money, we'd set up a band fund. At first we pooled most of what we made until we saved up enough to buy a secondhand PA system—speakers, monitors, a mixing board, microphones—beginning of junior year. It was a big investment, but it paid off over time, not having to rent equipment. Plus it was nice having a system we knew was reliable.

Once we bought the PA, we sliced the band fund cut to half, and split the other half five ways. I put most of my money into instruments, my growing guitar collection. At that point, I had the 355, a used Eric Clapton reissue Fender Stratocaster, a gorgeous Guild acoustic D40-C with a cutaway, plus a few hackaround guitars.

For the past two summers, we'd worked full time on an ice route, carting around five- and ten-pound bags of cubes and block ice to stock vending machines all over the county. Grocery and convenience stores, gas stations, yacht clubs (of which there are a lot along the Sound), country clubs. During the school year, we only worked two days a week, Wednesday afternoons and Saturdays. Once summer's over, the demand for ice drops.

"What do I think about what?" I locked the ice bay door and headed around for the passenger seat. It was Theo's turn to drive.

He hopped behind the wheel and started the engine, but didn't put the truck in gear.

"About Carey."

I considered the question, and, given Theo's obvious interest, looked for a diplomatic way to phrase my answer.

"She's different," I said, in a neutral tone. "Maybe living in another country does that to you."

Theo looked thoughtful as he slipped into reverse

and did a three-point turn. We rumbled over the gravel out of the parking lot.

I switched on the radio, which was tuned to WIGG, the classic rock station out of Newbridge. Two to six every day, Theo's favorite DJ was on, a manic megamouth who called himself the Headhunter. The Headhunter was spewing his normal spiel.

"Don't forget to feed your head, folks. And speaking of heads, I heard a story the other day."

I groaned. "Do we have to listen to this?" The Headhunter is notorious for dopey head jokes.

"Hey, Boog, this guy's on to something. He knows life is a state of mind. It's in your head." Theo reached over and turned up the volume.

". . . no body, just a head," the Headhunter blared into the cab of the truck. "So Head is born, but he adjusts well. Very independent-minded. Rolls to school every day, gets straight A's—great with oral reports—popular, good at team sports, especially soccer—"

Theo was already chuckling. Maybe you have to be a doctor's kid to appreciate that kind of grotesque body humor.

"One day Head's rolling home after school, and his fairy godmother appears.

"She says, 'Head, you've been so good. I'm going to grant you a wish.'

" 'Anything I want?' Head asks.

" 'You name it,' she says.

" 'Okay. I want to be a pickle.'

"The fairy godmother laughs. 'Excuse me,' she says, 'but I thought I heard you say you want to be a pickle.'

" 'That's what I said,' says Head.

" 'Head, you've got one wish—are you absolutely sure you want to be a pickle?' the fairy godmother asks.

" 'Absolutely,' says Head.

"The fairy godmother shrugs. 'I don't censor them, I just grant them.' So she waves her wand and presto, Head's a pickle. Then she disappears. A minute later, a hungry dog comes walking down the road. He sniffs the pickle, licks it, then gobbles it down.

"So folks, the moral of this story is—"

Theo chimed in, snickering. "Quit while you're a head."

THERE'S A SIMPLE formula for success in music: how good you get is directly proportional to how much you play. You want to get good, you practice; you want to stay good, you practice. True for solo players, true for bands. One of the reasons Blues Thing got so tight so fast was that besides playing out, we practiced every Monday and Thursday night, from seven to ten, and more when we could work it in.

Since my father was the only one of our collective set of parents who considered music a higher priority than sheltering the family vehicles from the elements, my garage was the place. Pop had helped me set it up as a studio of sorts, with sound-proof insulation so we could crank up good and loud. He also made sure the wiring was right, enough capacity to handle the juice from all our equipment, and properly grounded. "You ever see a guy glued to his guitar because the current's running through him? It's no joke. Don't fool around. When you play out, especially private parties, if you use a three-prong adaptor, make damn sure the ground wires are connected.''

My mother had donated the old brown couch from our den when she redecorated. We kept all our PA equipment in the garage, plus Keith's old drum kit, and a four-track cassette recorder I'd gotten for Christmas sophomore year. It was a decent setup.

When Theo showed up at practice the Monday of the third week of school, he seemed kind of glum. We warmed up with Freddie King's version of ''Hoochie Coochie Man,'' a tune Willie Dixon wrote for Muddy Waters, vintage blues. Given the level of energy Theo put out, to call our rendition subdued would be kind. To call it limp would be closer to the mark.

I looked at him. ''What?''

''Huh?'' he said. His mind was obviously elsewhere. ''Sorry, guys. The doctor's been on my case again.'' ''The doctor'' is what Theo always called his father. His mother did too. Dr. Stone has that kind of authoritative aura.

''The college thing?'' Danny asked. He noodled a few bars of the graduation march.

''Yeah.'' Theo flopped on the couch. ''How the hell am I supposed to know what I want to do for the rest of my life? I like to sing. That's what I like to do.''

''So why don't you apply to music school like Boog's doing?'' Danny turned to me. ''You get your application to Berklee in yet?''

I nodded. ''Two weeks ago.'' Berklee College of Music in Boston was my first choice. And really, the only place I wanted to go.

Theo looked even glummer. "Music school's not an option. He won't even discuss it. Says it's time I got serious." He gnawed on his thumbnail, and I could see it, a brainstorm coming over the horizon. "Hey Boog, about how much do we have in the band fund right now?"

"About three hundred twenty-seven dollars and forty-two cents," I told him. "Replacing that blown tweeter set us back some." I was in charge of maintaining our PA equipment.

"I was thinking," he said slowly. He looked around at each of us. "What if we started saving toward studio time? Go in, make a decent tape, one we could send out to agents, record companies? We could probably even sell copies locally at record stores, you know?"

"We already have a demo tape, Theo," Keith said. "It's enough to get us jobs around here."

"Yeah, but it's old. And the quality's pretty poor. No offense, Boog," he added quickly. I'd produced the other tape on my four track. "But, you know, it's not professional."

"What's the point in doing this now, Theo? I mean, Blues Thing's gonna be together for another year or so, but then we're all going away to school."

Theo looked pained at the thought. "Listen. At the least, it'd be a good thing to have under our belts—like a résumé thing. And what if we actually got offered a record contract? Wouldn't that be worth postponing college for a year, something that big? Do you think your folks would go for that, Boog?"

I thought about it. "Maybe. If it was a solid contract. And if it was what I really wanted to do. Would yours?"

He shrugged, looking uncertain and stubborn at the same time.

The other guys seemed ambivalent about the idea.

"It's a real long shot, Theo. And we'd need original material. We don't have anything original put together." Keith being practical, as usual. "No record company's gonna give us a contract strictly on covers."

"But say we had some tunes of our own—you guys be willing to give it a try?" Theo was in his best persuasive mode; good luck trying to resist.

"Yeah, I guess so," Danny said. Peter and Keith hesitated, then nodded, kind of neutrally. And I was game.

"I'll make some phone calls, find out what kind of money we're talking about," I said.

"Great. And I'll start working on some songs. Originals. I got a couple of ideas." He went a little mysterious when he said that. Then he started to chuckle about something.

"What?" I asked again.

"When the doctor told me I didn't take life seriously enough, I said, 'Well, Doctor, I look at it like this:' " He crossed his eyes, stuck his tongue out, and puffed up his cheeks, imitating Harpo Marx's gag goof-face.

We all cracked up, although I was betting it hadn't gone over so big with his father.

Theo was himself again, energized, completely recharged. He grabbed the mike.

"All right. It's all right." He sang it the second

time. " 'Jumpin' Jack Flash.' This Stone's ready to roll. Let's do it!"

The Friday night before the Harvest Dance, we weren't playing out, so we'd scheduled an extra practice. It was a typical Friday evening at my house: Charlie Parker, one of Pop's idols, on the stereo and a prefabricated dinner, pizza. My mother's usually pretty beat by the end of the week; being a part-time writer for the local alternative newspaper, she gets involved in a lot of causes. You name it, civil rights, gay rights, children's rights, prisoners' rights, general old human rights, even animal rights—Mom's a believer in rights and righting wrongs, and she doesn't stop at writing about them. She goes to meetings. She joins committees.

Also typical that night, my sister Allison pushing the outside of the parental control envelope, an activity she'd polished to an art form since turning fourteen.

"Mother, I need fifty dollars." Allie tossed it out with such panache, I had to chuckle.

Mom took a sip of Chianti, part of her TGIF winddown ritual, and came back with a variation of her standard response to statements like that.

"Why, when, to do what, where, with whom?"

Allie rolled her eyes and supplied the information, speaking slowly, with this sarcastic condescension, as if Mom had a comprehension disability.

"To take the train. Tomorrow. Where? New York City. The borough of Manhattan. To hang out, maybe do some shopping, hit a museum or something. Me, Jenny, and Sara. So, okay?"

"So, no, not okay," Mom said cheerfully.

"Why not?" The indignant sputter. "You let Him—" meaning me, a finger jab for emphasis, "—do Everything. You never let Me do Anything." Allie talks in capitals a lot. "You Said when I was in High School, I'd have more Freedom. You're always talking about Rights—what about Teenagers' rights? Why don't you Practice what you Preach?"

Mom shot Pop a look which I interpreted as a cue that it was time to take a united stand.

"Zip the lip, Allison. Your mother said no. Case closed." Pop has a pretty mild manner, but it camouflages an iron will.

I munched on a crust and watched Allie weigh her options. I could almost hear the conversation she was having with herself.

Is it worth the hassle of taking them both on? Probably not this time. Well, they said no to that, so they have to say yes to this next one.

She tossed her hair back and folded her arms. "Can we go to the mall then? And will you drive, both ways? Jenny's parents have a wedding and Sara's mother's busy. And can I still have the fifty dollars?"

Mom sipped her wine and smiled. She appreciates good technique, but she wasn't buying.

"Your mother is busy too. I can pick you up around six, but I can't drive you there. There's an open forum on the proposed expansion for the homeless shelter in the afternoon. And you got your allowance this week. If you need more money, you know where your bankbook is."

Allie pursed her lips, sighed through her nose, then threw her hands up in the air, just a few of the dramatic gestures in her repertoire. The doorbell signaled the end of the bout, which I scored as a TKO for Mom. Allie hopped up and beelined for the front door.

From the kitchen, I could hear Theo's greeting. "Hey, Allie-Oop. Where's Boog?" Allie-Oop was what he always called her. She used to be big-time into gymnastics, back flips, handsprings. If anyone else had called her that, Allie probably would have clocked them. From Theo, she just lapped up the attention like all the other women.

I checked the time. He was half an hour early, rare for him. A second later, he appeared in the kitchen doorway, holding Carey Harrigan's hand. Allie brought up the rear, looking as frigid as if someone had just dunked her in ice water.

"It's Theo and a Girl," she announced. "Ex-Cuse me. I have to go clean my Birdcage."

Allie doesn't have a bird; that's her code for blowing someone off. The few times Sharon called after trampling my finer feelings to ask why we couldn't be friends, Allie fielded the calls for me and that's what she told her: "He can't come to the phone; he's cleaning his birdcage." Allie took off for her room. Theo seemed oblivious to the snub.

When he introduced Carey to my parents, she kind of hung back, nodding shyly but not saying a word, until she spotted this huge jungly plant hanging over the sink.

Now my mother's good at a lot of things. The one exception is plants. She says it stems back to second grade, when hers was the only scarlet runner bean that didn't sprout in the paper cup. Philodendrons get terminal jaundice at our house. The ficus tree we gave her for the den immediately developed an acute case of leaf drop.

"Look at that. It hates me," Mom had said.

"You're supposed to Talk to your plants, Mother," Allie told her.

So she talked to it. Remarks like, "Don't you droop your branches at me, you ugly twig."

This plant over the sink was an anomaly. It didn't die, but it didn't do what it was supposed to either. As soon as Carey saw it, she stepped over to the sink.

"Bougainvillea," she said.

"Is that what it is?" Mom said. "I just wanted something with flowers. This is what they sold me; they said it would flower year round. It hasn't flaunted a single petal all summer."

"Did you repot it after you bought it?" Carey asked, lifting up the overgrowth and peering underneath.

Mom blinked. "Why, yes. I did. It wasn't a cheap pot, either. In fact, I've done more for that plant than for any other plant I've ever had. Water. Drops. New pot. My sunniest window. And this is how it repays me."

Carey smiled, kind of timidly. "That might be the problem. It looks overpotted." She started talking faster, her words spilling out over each other. "See, they like to be potbound. If you put it in one that's too big, you're almost guaranteed to overwater and overfeed it. And that'll make the foliage grow like anything, but you won't get any flowers." She stopped talking, out of breath.

"You mean I've been taking too good care of it?" Mom sounded flabbergasted.

Now Carey laughed and seemed to relax a bit. "Kind of. Try letting it dry out, really wilt it, but not dead. Then give it a good water and after that, wilt it again, maybe two more times. It should pop buds for you. You can get it to bloom year round, but it needs dormant periods, a few months in between."

"Well." Mom was shaking her head. "What do you think of that?"

Pop chuckled. "Sounds like your kind of plant, Jeannie. Water it once a month whether it needs it or not."

Theo and Carey sat down while Mom cleared away the pizza and put on coffee. Carey didn't take off her army jacket or her hat either, an oversized maroon beret. It occurred to me then that I'd never seen her without a hat and I wondered if maybe she had a bald spot or something. She had a flowery cloth bag kind of thing with her, that she was clutching like it contained the crown jewels. I could see a rectangular, notebook-sized outline pressed against the fabric.

"Anyone for dessert? Cannolis from Angelo's Bakery. Theo, you love these. Everyone, help yourself." Mom set the foil platter in the middle of the table, along with freshbrewed coffee, then sat down herself.

"So Carey, does a green thumb run in your family?"

Mom's investigative technique. I knew the question was designed to elicit some info about Carey's background, without seeming nosy.

The question seemed to fluster Carey. "Uh, well, I don't know," she murmured. "I just like plants."

"Carey's father's a botanist," Theo put in. He slipped an arm around her shoulders and smiled at

40

her. "They've been living in Brazil—he was cataloging rain forest stuff and—"

"Excuse me, could I use your bathroom, please?" Carey said suddenly, pushing her chair back, in the process knocking Theo's arm away and standing up, but not meeting anyone's eyes.

Theo looked startled.

"Down the hall," Mom said. She pointed and smiled. As Carey left the room, my mother was looking after her curiously. "What did you say Carey's last name was, Theo?"

"Harrigan," Theo told her. "She and her father are renting a place up in Yardley Hills, until they can find one of their own. I guess Mr. Harrigan's looking for a teaching job at a university down in the city."

Mom nodded. She had a thoughtful look on her face, the one that usually signals that she's pulled a pertinent fact out of her mental archives, but she didn't ask Carey any more questions. She took her coffee out to the den to catch the evening news, while Pop went off to go through his Friday night pregig rituals. Theo popped a third cannoli in his mouth, then snapped his fingers.

"Damn, I forgot it."

"Forgot what?"

He swallowed. "New CD I want to play for you guys. Neville Brothers. Man, what a voice—Aaron Neville—"

Carey came back into the kitchen. Theo hopped up and put a hand on her shoulder.

"Listen. I have to run back to the house to get something," he said.

"I'll come—" she started to say.

41

"Stay. Eat dessert. I'll be right back."

He was out the door before she could say anything else. I had the feeling he wanted us to get better acquainted. As the front door slammed, Carey sat back down.

"Your family seems really nice," she said, tentatively. I was caught by this wistfulness in her voice.

"Thanks." My wheels were spinning, trying to get a reading on this strange woman. "Want some?" I pushed the plate of pastries over to her.

She shook her head. I got up and started to clear the rest of the stuff off the table. Allie flounced in while I was rinsing the soda cans, grabbed two cannolis from the counter where I'd put them, then flounced out again without saying a word.

Carey raised an eyebrow nervously at me, and I felt the need to apologize for my sister's lack of hospitality.

"Sorry about Allie. She's always had kind of a thing for Theo."

Now she smiled, almost sympathetically. "I can see why," she said. "He's pretty special."

"Yeah," I said. "He is."

Carey seemed like she wanted to say something else, but it took her a minute to get it out.

"Listen, Boog, I hope you don't mind that I tagged along tonight."

"No problem," I said. I grabbed the sponge to wipe down the table. Actually, I did have a slight problem with it. Her presence felt intrusive to me somehow, and I wished Theo had mentioned it in advance, because I would have voted in the negative. I didn't like an audience when we practiced, and the general policy was not to bring girlfriends along. Too distracting, for one thing.

I tossed the sponge in the sink and headed for the door to the breezeway.

"We can wait out there for Theo and the other guys," I said, without looking her in the eye. Something about Carey's story was bugging me, like a false note in a tune.

chapter 4

WHEN I GOT my license, end of sophomore year, Pop got himself a new work van and gave me his old blue one. Sixty-three thousand miles and the air conditioning didn't work, but it was big enough to cart the band's equipment around and it was dependable, especially compared to the wheels Theo got as a hand-me-down. Theo's ten-year-old Saab was rustier than a sunken battleship, about as reliable as a dead mailman, and if it had been a horse, it would have been long gone to the glue factory. He was saving as much money as he could hang on to toward the down payment on a new car.

Anyhow, we covered the sides of the van, where it said Buglioni Electric, with Blues Thing bumper stickers, and whenever we had a gig scheduled, Theo always hoofed it down to my house to pack up the PA and we'd go together.

Late afternoon the day of the Harvest Dance, last Saturday in September, Theo called to say he'd meet me over at school. No explanation, just, "Can you handle packing the van yourself? I'll be there to help you unload.'' I said fine, but I wondered what had precipitated the change in routine.

Allie asked me if I could pick up her friend Sara and drop them both at Jenny's house, so they could get ready and go together. Seeking strength in numbers for their first major high-school social function. I said sure. Allie and Mom had engaged in a minor skirmish earlier over what she was and was not allowed to wear in public: She could not wear the skintight blue jeans with the hole worn in the butt so her flowered underwear showed through; she could not wear the black see-through shirt, which if my mother had known she was buying, she would have told Allie not to waste her money; she could not wear her bathing suit top under a lace leotard—although she could wear the leotard with a jumper over it, that's what it was for.

It seemed to me that after a few protests, Allie had accepted Mom's fashion decrees in an unusually docile manner. As she hopped in the car with a stuffed knapsack, her whole scheme became clear to me: leave the house in an approved outfit, and change clothes at Jenny's. I shrugged. I wasn't going to bug the kid. I'd be there to keep an eye on her.

"Seat belt," I said automatically. "You're never going to get your license if you don't start remembering. It's the first thing they check. If you don't buckle up, you're outta there."

"Yes, Big Brother." Allie yanked the shoulder strap over and jammed it into the clasp. "Where's Theo? He always goes with you." She faked a small yawn, a show at being blasé.

I turned the key in the ignition and nursed the engine to a steady idle. "I don't know. He said he'd meet me there."

"Oh," she said. I could tell she was disappointed.

We were about halfway down the street when she came out with one of those intuitive flashes, like my mother does sometimes. It took me by surprise, made me realize she was really growing up.

"I bet it's that girl. That Carey person." But she didn't say it with the same hostility she'd exhibited the night Theo brought Carey over. In fact, she sounded so deflated, I snuck a glance. She was staring out the window and it appeared that there might be some actual heartache going on. Another surprise.

"Hey," I said when we stopped at the corner.

"Hey what?" She didn't look at me.

"Carey's pretty strange. Flaky. It probably won't last." Somehow I didn't believe it. I don't think Allie did either. But she forced a smile.

"Thanks anyway, Big Brother." She sighed. I had an impulse to pat her on the head, but I resisted it; Allie's not the touchy-feely type.

Theo's Saab burped and lurched into the parking space next to mine, in the back lot behind the gym, just as I was unloading the last of our equipment. Allie's hunch had been right on the money. Carey was in the passenger seat. They both got out and strolled over to me. Theo was wearing his favorite vest, a black suede deal, over a T-shirt painted to look like a tux, and faded black jeans. And Carey was dressed in her usual miscellaneous style—a paisley scarf tied like a tie around her neck, over a black turtleneck, a tweed blazer three sizes too big, the most patched over blue jeans I'd ever seen, and the inevitable hat, this time a limp brown felt fedora.

I was a little irritated Theo was late. It's not professional, and that's one of the things Pop's hammered into me: If they're paying you, you better be professional. Setting up was a lot of work, a cooperative effort. Even though Theo didn't have an instrument of his own to deal with, he always pulled his weight. But a few times recently, he'd been a bit of a slacker, as if his mind was elsewhere. From the looks of things, it was going to be a slacker night, grunt-workwise.

"Glad you could make it," I said. The irony seemed lost on Theo at that moment.

"It's gonna be a good night," he said. "I can feel it." He was moving to some mental rhythm, smiling at Carey, like he was singing a song inaudible except to her. Much as I hated to interrupt such a Hallmark moment, I shoved a milk crate full of mikes and power cords toward him.

"Wanna go help the guys plug in and tape down the wires, please?"

"No sweat," Theo said. "Coming?" he said to Carey, who was slouching inside her jacket, as if she sensed she was a contributing factor to my annoyance, by virtue of being a distraction to Theo.

"Yep," she said. She slipped an arm around his waist. He adjusted the milk crate in one arm, put the other around her shoulders and they headed for the gym, almost as one unit. It gave me this feeling that there was no need or room for anyone else in either of their lives. I took a deep breath and waited outside for a few minutes to get into my own music mood, then went in.

The Harvest Dance was a sellout. Wall-to-wall bodies. Natalie and her committee had gone all out with the decorations. Leaves were strewn all over the floor, pumpkins and gourds artfully scattered along the sides, orange, red, and yellow streamers strung like vines from the ceiling, a genuine haystack was under one of the basketball nets, a scarecrow was hanging from one of the climbing ropes, and taking up a big chunk of the back wall, was a huge brown paper cornucopia with purple and green balloons spilling out, like giant grapes.

The white noise of the gathering crowd built steadily while we tuned up. Eight o'clock on the nose, Theo blasted through it.

"Is everybody ready to party?"

He didn't have to ask twice like he did some nights. The crowd came back with one roaring "Yeah!" as we launched into the Allman Brothers' "One Way Out."

It's always interesting being up on stage in your own territory. You look down at the sea of people, kids you pass in the hall every day. Here and there, a particular face will pop out at you. I caught sight of Allie huddling with her friends near the bleachers. And Sharon with her new squeeze. I gauged my reaction to seeing her with another guy and was relieved to realize the worst was definitely over. It didn't bother me. She wiggled her fingers when we made eye contact, and I even managed a minor smile.

The whole first set, Carey leaned against the stage near one of our speakers, at the front of the dance floor area. Kids were dancing around her, bumping into her, but she didn't seem to notice. Even though she was right in the middle of the crowd, she seemed set apart from it somehow. I watched her, watched kids notice her, and looks would cross their faces, especially the girls, that seemed to say, "You're not one of us." She didn't seem to notice or care. She was into the music. And into Theo. And it was obviously mutual.

We wound up the set with "Tuff Enuff," a modern song, but classic, by the Fabulous Thunderbirds, with Stevie Ray's big brother Jimmie on guitar. You know a song's a classic when you can take it in your head and imagine any one of the greats doing his own cover version of it. The guitar tremolo rolls the rhythm along like a funky snake, and it's one of those tunes that always gets people moving, and keeps them charged up for the next set.

Carey was dancing by herself, a slinky, gyrating swaying kind of thing. Theo was kneeling on the edge of the stage, crooning it right to her. Between the two of them, the number got so hot I half-expected one of the chaperons to come over with a fire extinguisher and hose them both down.

Toward the end of the number, Natalie Stewart worked her way to the front of the dance floor, with a guy I hadn't seen around school in tow, a molded-muscle, sun-lamp tan type, with bristly blond hair. At that point, Carey's and Theo's little exhibition was drawing some attention. The guy whispered something to Natalie, and a kind of smirk, half scornful, half self-congratulatory, came over her face, like she'd just had a suspicion of hers confirmed.

We finished up the set.

"We're gonna take a short break now, people. Keep the party pumping. Yeah!" Theo slipped his mike back into the stand and turned to me. He was dripping sweat already; his brand of vocals was a full-tilt workout.

"I'm gonna go wipe down and change my shirt. Keep Carey company till I get back?"

I nodded, thinking I'd never seen him this protective with a woman before, unstrapped my guitar, and set it out of harm's way, while Theo ducked through the wings to the backstage men's room. I moseyed over to the edge of the stage and sat next to where Carey was standing. She gave me a tentative smile.

"So what'd you think?" I asked.

She opened her mouth, then closed it into a smile, and gave a shake of her head, like she didn't have words superlative enough. It had been a great set, I knew by the way I was still mentally gliding in the groove. As a unit, the band was tight, and my solos were as smooth as they ever get. I could tell that as a listener, Carey had picked up on the nuances, which is always gratifying. I smiled back at her, feeling the most comfortable I'd felt with her so far.

Natalie chose that moment to intrude.

"Hi, Boog. Four hundred thirty-two tickets, final count. So you guys'll get six hundred forty-eight dollars."

"Great," I said.

She wasn't finished. "Oh, by the way, this is Allan Rappoport. He's captain of Clifton's football team."

Clifton is a town down the Sound, about halfway between Yardley and the New York border, maybe thirty miles away.

"Carey, you know Allan, don't you?"

Carey had gone paler than usual, except for two pink blotches on her cheeks.

Natalie lunged onward. Her fangs were showing.

"Sure you do."

The guy Allan looked kind of shamefaced, like he'd been shanghaied into participating in a dirty deed. Natalie kept talking.

"See, Allan knows Carey from school. Her father used to teach biology there, until he got fired last year. So I guess that story about boarding school in Brazil was a big load of bull twinkies."

Carey didn't react, didn't move. Natalie had apparently scored a direct hit, but I guess that wasn't enough; she went for a blitzkrieg.

"Pretty pathetic—falling down drunk in front of a class."

I couldn't take any more.

"Hey Natalie, you're about as subtle as a train wreck, you know that?"

Allan had been standing there staring at his shoes, but his conscience must have started poking him, because he grabbed Natalie's arm and worked her away into the crowd.

Carey was just standing there, staring off into space.

"Hey," I said, putting a hand on her shoulder. She looked at me, her expression totally flat.

"Why did you lie?" I couldn't think of anything else to say. Even though I'd stuck up for her, it bothered me. A lot. Lying's probably one of the things I hate most. It's hard enough figuring out life without having people deliberately sabotage your figuring with bullshit. Besides which, I felt like it really made Theo look like a fool.

She shrugged her shoulders slowly.

Then Theo was back, freshened up for the next set, wearing a T-shirt that said, "We are the people our parents warned us about."

"What's up?" he asked immediately. The change in Carey's demeanor was pretty radical.

She shot me a scared glance, like she thought I was going to blow her cover then and there. I gave my head a tiny shake. I thought she should tell him, hoped she would. But it wasn't my secret to spill, although with Natalie knowing, I suspected it wouldn't be a secret for long.

"I'm a little tired," she told him. "Can I just sit in the wings and listen?"

Theo put his arm around her. "You can do anything you want to do."

For the rest of the night, Carey sat tucked behind the stage curtains, alternating between listening, and writing another chapter, I assumed, in Volume VII of her life.

SOME PEOPLE ARE tougher to decipher than others. Carey was in that category. There were times when she was so up, you almost felt like you should tie a few sandbags to her shoes. Other times, a kind of depression hovered around her, like a cloud so thick you could practically see it.

Thursday was current events day in World Studies, quiz day, basically on all the woes of the world; seems like that's the bulk of the news. The week after the Harvest Dance, *Time* had featured world hunger, with an emphasis on, but not limited to, famine in developing countries. There were a lot of insert boxes and photographs of starving people, kids ravaged by malnutrition, more than I could look at and then comfortably go sit down to one of my mother's pasta dinners.

It was one of Carey's cloud days. Before the bell rang, she turned to Theo.

"Ironic isn't it?" She held up the *Time*. "Nice contrast with harvest and homecoming."

Theo rubbed the top of her hat du jour, a tan wool golf cap. "Hey, you can't absorb all this stuff."

She shook her head dejectedly. "No. You're right. I can't. But how do you block it out?" She turned back around in her seat without waiting for an answer. Theo leaned his chin on his hand, staring at her, like he was trying to see inside her mind.

Brockmeyer popped the quiz as soon as we sat down. She wrote it on the board: "LIST THE FOLLOWING: 1. Three causes of food shortages. 2. Three countries in which starvation threatens the survival of a population. 3. Three effects of severe malnutrition on children. 4. Three solutions which could alleviate some of the hunger in the world.

"Take out a piece of loose-leaf. You have ten minutes."

Typical Brockmeyer, go for specifics, cut through the euphemisms, get to the meat of the matter. I'd only skimmed the magazine, because it was such a grim issue. I jotted down what I could remember, then sat back, figuring I'd chalked up my first F of the year.

We passed the quizzes in, and Brockmeyer stuck the stack on her desk under a book.

"All right, now. There are food resources enough at this point in time to feed every human being on the planet. So why are people starving to death?"

As Brockmeyer waited for answers, Carey stood quietly, pulled the brim of her cap down over her forehead, picked up her things, and walked toward the door.

Brockmeyer's jaw dropped, then snapped back.

"Excuse me, Miss Harrigan, do you have a more

pressing engagement elsewhere?'' Her tone was tempered steel.

Carey turned back for a second. I tried to read the expression on her face. She looked sad to the point of being sick, like she'd been forced to swallow something her stomach just couldn't handle.

"No, I don't," she said.

"Would it be presumptuous of me to inquire why you're walking out of my class?" Miss Brockmeyer asked sarcastically.

Theo was leaning forward in his seat, frowning with concern. Carey shot him a glance I couldn't interpret, then looked back at Brockmeyer, almost absentmindedly.

"Read my quiz," she said softly. And left.

The room was so still you could have heard a mosquito blink. Brockmeyer stood like a statue, looking at the door. I think she was truly amazed. After a moment, she just turned back to the rest of us.

"Why are people starving to death?" she repeated.

It was a depressing class, due to the subject matter. I was glad when it was over and was high-tailing toward the door, when Brockmeyer's voice pulled me back.

"James Buglioni, could I see you for a minute?"

I searched my brain to see if any immediate screwups came to mind, but no red flags popped out. Theo gave me a quick absentminded wave and bolted. I didn't have to guess where he was going—off to track down Carey.

I fought the flood of exiting kids back to Brockmeyer's desk and stood there, putting on my blandest poker face as a precaution.

"I was one of the chaperons at the Harvest Dance. I really enjoyed your performance," she said, smiling up at me.

I found the comment intensely peculiar, coming from Miss Brockmeyer. It made me wary. Was she a closet Blues Thing groupie?

"Thanks," I said.

"You're quite an accomplished guitarist. Have you been playing long?" If this conversation was going somewhere, I needed a guidebook.

"Thanks," I repeated. "A little over five years."

Brockmeyer smiled again, as if she recognized my bewilderment and was ready to clear it up.

"Have you ever heard of Anchor House?"

I shook my head.

"It's a youth shelter over in Newbridge. The Council of Churches runs it, for kids who have severe family problems and need a place to stay. I'm involved with recreational activities for the residents." She paused.

I had no clue what the proper response was, so I winged it.

"That's, uh, very commendable."

Now she laughed. "I'll get to the point. We have a resident who's been there for a few weeks. He's fourteen. His name is Charlie, and for the most part, he's been pretty withdrawn."

I nodded cautiously, still basically in the dark.

"Someone donated a used guitar to Anchor House. When Charlie saw it, it was the first time he exhibited any kind of interest, any real spark. And an idea occurred to me at the dance, when your band was playing. Is there any chance you'd be willing to show him a few things on the guitar? Give him a lesson or two, just get him started and see if it leads anywhere?''

I stammered and stuttered for a moment, cleared my throat, scratched my head, and shuffled my feet while I thought about the request. Brockmeyer waited, and I could tell if I said no for some reason, she wouldn't hold it against me. My hesitation wasn't because I didn't want to help out a kid with a rough life; I think it was more the idea of that kind of involvement seeming like a big responsibility. I mean, what if it didn't work out and this kid ended up worse off than he was, feeling like a failure? For some reason, what Carey'd said at lunch that first day came into my mind, about how she'd rather dream about doing something than find out she couldn't. It struck me as the ultimate excuse never to stick your neck out, and kind of made me feel like I had an obligation to give this kid's dream a boost.

''Sure,'' I said. ''I'll give it a try.''

''Good.'' Suddenly, Brockmeyer was all business again, but it seemed like there was a little twinkle of approval in her eyes. ''How about this Sunday? Is that a good day for you?''

I was really in it now. ''Uh, yeah, I guess so. In the afternoon's okay. We have to play out Saturday night so—''

''Fine. I'll write out directions and give them to you in class tomorrow.'' She nodded at me. Dismissed.

*   *   *

I didn't see either Theo or Carey at lunchtime or for the rest of the day. I called Theo at home that night, to confirm some things about our gig, and to run some possibilities for new material by him.

"Where'd you disappear to today, anyway?" I said.

When he answered, it was slowly. "Carey was kind of down. We went for a drive, up to Devil's Hollow."

Devil's Hollow is right below the Pequot Reservoir, on the northernmost edge of town. The Pequot River runs down from the dam, through Hydraulic Company runoff land, cuts across town, and runs into the Mohegan River just below the parkway. There's a series of waterfalls and pools, carved out of the rock by the water, called the Cascades. Depending on the overflow from the reservoir, it can be intense. It's all surrounded by these mammoth boulders that kids jump off. Strictly illegal, and pretty dangerous; if the Yardley cops even catch you up there with wet clothes, they write you a ticket. I'd actually never made the leap from the top, always went off one of the lower ledges. I'm not big on heights. Theo did it all the time, no sweat, from Devil's Ledge, the highest rock.

"Oh," I said.

Something inside me felt a little funny, like, intruded upon. Not that Devil's Hollow was my own private hideaway, or anything, but it was mostly a place where the guys went. If anyone wanted to go for a swim, there was no worrying about stripping down and jumping in; that way, if the cops came, your clothes wouldn't be wet. Anyhow, it was sort of an unspoken understanding that we took girls to Colford P. Worthington Park and kept the Hollow to ourselves.

"What was she upset about?" I asked.

Again Theo hesitated, as if he didn't want to reveal a confidence. "I think all that stuff in *Time*, the starving people, got to her."

The next day, Brockmeyer handed back our quizzes. When she gave Carey hers, I didn't detect the usual contempt in her manner. She looked like she understood something a little better.

"This is not the right answer to the quiz questions or to the problems they addressed." She didn't mention Carey's having gone AWOL from class the day before.

I saw a red F on the top of Carey's paper as she slipped it in her book. I myself squeaked by with a D+.

At lunch, I crashed Carey and Theo's twosome in the far corner of the courtyard.

"Mind if I join you?" I asked. Theo shoved over on the bench. Carey smiled at me. I started in on my cold-cuts combo. I wasn't going to say anything, but my curiosity was bugging me like a big lint lump inside the toe of my sock—I could live with it, but I'd be a lot more comfortable if I got it out.

"Can I ask you something?" I said to Carey.

"What?" she said.

"I was just wondering what you wrote on your quiz. I mean, Brockmeyer seemed to back off. I was expecting her to give you the mincemeat treatment after yesterday."

Carey looked at me like she was weighing something. Then she reached into her knapsack, pulled out the quiz, and held it out. I took it and scanned it. It was a poem, or part of one.

Come away, O human child!
To the waters and the wild
With a faery, hand in hand,
For the world's more full of weeping than you can
  understand.

"Hmmmm," I said, for lack of a more pertinent comment. Someone else turning in a poem for a quiz might have seemed pretentious. But it didn't come across that way from Carey.

"It's by Yeats, 'The Stolen Child,' " Theo told me.

I handed her back the paper and she stuffed it in her bag. To be honest, I didn't know quite what to make of it. But it obviously said something to Theo. Sitting there with the two of them, the way they were looking at each other, I felt pretty superfluous.

That Sunday, I showed up at Anchor House about 2:30. It was a big old Victorian house in a tough section of Newbridge, down by the waterfront. Fifty years ago or so, it must have been a nice neighborhood, judging from the houses. But it had gone down the urban decay tubes, like a lot of the city. Anchor House itself looked like an oasis of security. A tall chain link fence surrounded the property, with locks on the gates to the front walk and the driveway. And it also looked like the one house on the street that people cared about. The paint wasn't chipping, the lawn was mowed, and there was a huge old ship's anchor, painted black, on the front lawn.

I'd called ahead, which Miss Brockmeyer told me to do, and the person I spoke to asked for a description of my car, and my license plate. I guess they were on the lookout for me, because as I pulled up the driveway gate, the front door opened.

A tall man wearing jeans and a warm-up jacket came out to meet me. He had a neat beard and tinted, gold-rimmed aviator-shaped glasses. He looked a little like Sonny Rollins, another one of Pop's idols. He unlocked the gate, and I drove around to the small parking lot behind the house. The man waited while I parked and got myself and my guitar out of the van, then introduced himself.

"Mac Winters. Thanks for coming, James."

We shook hands.

As we walked around to the front door, Mac filled me in a little on the kid's background.

"Charlie's the oldest of three kids. His father had a drug problem, walked out after the youngest was born, hasn't been heard from since. His mother has an abusive boyfriend, who's been living with them, off and on. Charlie had a run-in with him. We got the call from the doctor at Newbridge Hospital emergency room. Eleven stitches on his forehead. He's been here for a month now. The other kids are in foster homes for the time being, but there wasn't a suitable foster situation for Charlie. The mother's still with the boyfriend."

Mac opened the door with a key from a big ring, and then dead bolted it behind us once we were inside.

He saw me looking at all the locks on the door, and his key ring.

"We don't try to lock the kids in. We try to lock the danger out. This is the first secure environment a lot of our residents have ever experienced. The anchor is the symbol for hope. I guess that's a good part of what we try to instill here."

There was a desk in the foyer with a phone and some accounting-type books. Mac had me sign in, giving me a brief rundown of the place.

"Main house rules—contribute to the community while you live here. No drinking, no drugs. A lot of the kids who come in have substance abuse problems. We make a pact with them—while they're here, they stay off the stuff."

"Must be tough to make that stick."

Mac nodded. "We get them into rehab if they need it. Surprisingly, it's not the worst problem for some of the kids. The psychological baggage some of them carry is more than anyone, especially a kid, should have to live with. We try and give them a chance to see there are other ways of living than what they've grown up with. That's about the best we can do. We're not a long-term facility—three months max, three weeks average stay. Once in awhile, we make an exception."

While he talked, Mac gave me a quick tour of the downstairs. The inside of the house was as well-kept as the outside. There was a lot of varnished wood paneling, and it had an old-timey feel. Solid, secure. The walls of the place projected it. We wound up in a small sitting room.

"I'll go get Charlie. Be right back."

At the doorway, he stopped and turned around, a furrow of worry over his eyebrows.

"He'll test you, you know. Try to put you off. Don't let him."

The furniture in the room looked old, donated I was guessing, but again, everything was neat as a pin. In one corner of the room was an old Martin guitar case. I went over to check it out. The guitar wasn't in bad shape; all those old Martins have beautiful tone. There were a few nicks in the finish, and a slight warp in the neck, because someone had not only strung it with really heavy gauge strings, they'd tuned it up a half step too high, and that kind of tension was too much for the guitar. The strings were farther away from the fretboard than you want them. It'd be pretty tough for a beginner. So I pulled out my needle-nose pliers from my case and a set of extra light gauge strings I'd brought along for just such a contingency, and started to restring it.

While I was working, Mac returned, kind of herding a thin kid in baggy khaki pants and a denim shirt in front of him. Straight black hair hung down over his forehead, but I could see a section of dark raw scar over his left eye. He was wearing a scowl that would have done a bulldog proud.

"Charlie, this is James Buglioni. James, Charlie Elliot." The kid stuck out his chin and gave me a cool once-over.

Mac winked at me over Charlie's shoulder. Then he backed out and closed the door.

Charlie sat down in the chair across from me, folded his arms across his skinny chest, and stretched out his legs, like he was bored to the bone already.

"So what do I call you? Mr. Buglioni? Sir? James?" He kind of sneered my name.

"My friends call me Boog—short for Boogie Man," I said as I took the last string out of its paper envelope.

"Oh, yeah?" he said. "Why's that? You got bad habits or something?"

"Huh?" I looked up from what I was doing. The kid was giving me an extremely hairy eyeball.

"Kid used to be in my class, everyone called him Booger King."

"Oh, yeah?" I said. "Why's that?"

"From all the nose souvenirs he wiped on his desk. End of every year, they had to sand it down."

His chin was out, his shoulders were tense, and he kept swiping his hair off his forehead, but it kept flopping back. He looked like he was ready to take me on. Somehow, combined with the scar over his eye, it kind of got to me. I didn't take the bait, just handed him the restrung guitar and took my own out of the case.

I'd brought an acoustic so I didn't have to drag an amp along, my Guild, a magnificent guitar, with a tone as golden as its cedar top, rich and mellow. I stuck a thumbpick on my right thumb, and launched into "Boogie Man," really hotdogging the solo to throw a little respect into the kid. He didn't take his eyes off my fingers the whole time. When I finished, he was quiet for a minute. Some of the bantam rooster pugnaciousness seemed to have subsided. He nodded, gnawed his lip, then like he'd tipped his hand, revealed too much, he came out with another crack.

"Your singing stinks. You been gargling with battery acid, or what?"

This time I just laughed. It's not that I can't carry a tune; I do harmonies sometimes when I'm playing an easy rhythm thing. But I can't sing at the same time as I'm really concentrating on playing.

"Pay attention. I'll show you something." I handed him a plastic flatpick.

The first thing I showed him was the box scale, a five-tone blues scale, 1, flat 3, 4, 5, flat 7 in a three-octave run up the neck. With those five notes and a few passing tones, you can say just about all there is to say about being sad or lonely, that howl-at-the-moon kind of feeling, the blues. I thought it might come in handy for a kid with problems. We went over alternate picking and some note values. Then I taught him three chords, A7, D7, and E7, the basic blues progression, I, IV, V, in the key of A.

He was sucking on his fingertips, scowling, after about an hour.

"Had enough?" I asked him.

Chin out again, like I'd insulted his manhood. The kid was a walking, talking attitude. "I'll let you know when I've had enough. Show me how to do that 'Boogie Man' thing."

I grinned. "Ever hear the story about the old man and the mule?"

Charlie fell for it, just like I had. I got him on the punchline, then went to sock him on the arm, the way Pop does with me.

Big mistake.

He dropped the guitar on the floor, sprang up, and squared off. His face went white, and his eyes looked like a wild animal's—fearful and blazing with rage at the same time.

"Don't touch me, you fat scumwad!" he screamed.

I was so stunned I jerked back in my chair, almost tipping it over. Mac was in the room in a second, his arms around Charlie from behind, restraining him. My tongue had turned to cement in my mouth. I couldn't have spoken even if I'd been able to think of something to say. Mac wrestled Charlie out of the room.

I sat there feeling dumber than dirt. I picked up the Martin and put it in the case. Mac came back while I was packing up my guitar.

"What set him off?" he asked.

I explained, trying to make it clear that I hadn't been threatening him, that it was only a gesture. "I guess he took it the wrong way. I'm sorry."

Mac nodded sympathetically. "Don't feel bad. There was no way for you to realize." He shook his head, looking kind of discouraged, and walked me back out to the parking lot, neither of us saying anything until I was in the driver's seat, ready to reverse, back out the way I'd come and leave it at that, literally and figuratively. The little bum had struck a nerve I'd thought was dead when he called me fat. I didn't need the aggravation.

Mac put his hand on the door before I closed it. "You'll come again, won't you, James? Charlie hasn't had anything he could count on for a long time."

If you don't swim so great, you stay out of deep water. Makes sense, right? This was way over my head. Tell him no, my rational side was saying calmly. My mouth didn't listen.

"Yeah, I guess so," was what came out.

chapter

6

THEO SNAGGED ME after school in the parking lot, the second Thursday in October.

"Hey, Boog, can I grab a lift?"

"No problem. Saab die again?" I got in, moved some junk off the passenger seat and tossed it and my books into the back.

Theo climbed in the other side, looking completely disgusted.

"In a coma, anyway. Battery, maybe. Won't turn over. It's always something. How am I supposed to save money for a new car when I have to keep pouring it into repairs for that piece of crap?"

He had my sympathy. Pop gives me a hand with funds now and then, and I only have to pay half my insurance. The doctor was tough.

I eased into the logjam of exiting traffic. Theo seemed preoccupied and restless. He kept drumming his fingers on the dashboard.

"Listen, can you drop me off at Carey's?" he asked abruptly, as I swung out onto the Post Road.

Carey hadn't been in school that day. Considering it was only the beginning of the second month of school, she'd been absent a lot. And half the time, it seemed like only her body was present. More often than not in class, she'd be scribbling in that composition book, which she got away with because the teachers assumed she was taking notes. It looked to me like she was filtering everything that happened through her pen.

"Sure," I said. "Where to?"

"North Road."

I couldn't help registering a touch of skepticism; you don't think of a fired school teacher as being able to afford to rent on North Road.

Theo picked up on what I was thinking.

"Listen, Boog, about her father—and saying they lived in Brazil—"

He must have known I knew, with the output from Natalie's rumor mill, but this was the first time the subject had come up between us. He sounded so uncomfortable, I cut him right off.

"She tell you herself?"

"Yeah." He frowned. "I don't know why she thought she had to lie. To me, I mean."

I took a right on Copper Beech Avenue and headed up toward Yardley Hills.

"Maybe she was embarrassed. Or maybe, you know, if he's trying to make a new start, she thought she was protecting him or something."

That slant seemed to make him feel a little better.

"What's the deal with her mother, anyway?" I'd only heard Carey mention her father, and I'd been meaning to ask.

"She's not around."

"Not around? What does that mean? Divorced? Dead?"

"I'm not sure," he said.

I gave him a sideways glance. He was chewing on his thumbnail.

"I'd like to buy a vowel, please," I said in a perplexed game show contestant tone. "You mean to tell me you've been going out with Carey for a month now and you don't know if her mother is divorced or dead?"

"Look, she hasn't told me, I haven't asked. I really don't give a shit what her father did, or where her mother is. I just care about her. When she's ready to tell me, she'll tell me." He was getting a little hot and bothered, so I backed off.

"Hey, it's none of my business." I stepped on the gas.

It was a gorgeous day, with the leaves just beginning to turn. The farther north on Copper Beech you go, the hillier it gets. From the top, you can see all of Yardley stretched out, and beyond it, the Sound all the way over to Long Island. When we got to the intersection with North Road, Theo pointed left. He seemed to be in a brooding kind of mood, rare for him. Normally what was on his mind came right out his mouth.

"So, you think Carey's sick?" I asked.

He didn't answer my question, just shrugged and frowned.

A Mercedes and a Jag passed us, going the other direction.

"Take a right at the end of that stone wall." He

pointed at the driveway of a property with an enormous brick monstrosity set back from the road.

"Wow. That's some house!" I was shocked.

At that, he gave me a half smile. "Go around back."

I followed the driveway, past a fork that led to a semicircle in front of the mansion, looped the van around a minirotary with a dry fountain in the middle of it, and headed toward the rear of the property.

"Over there."

I pulled up to what looked like the main house's bastard offspring, and I had to chuckle. It was something straight out of the Brothers Grimm. Somehow it seemed to fit Carey perfectly.

"It's the caretaker's cottage," Theo told me. "I guess Mr. Harrigan has some kind of deal on the rent—the owners are down in Palm Beach for the winter and he's watching over the grounds."

"Is that all he does? Does he have another job? How do they live?" My curiosity was surprising me.

"He works for some plant nursery. So it wasn't a total lie, the botanist bit. Plants are his thing." Theo sounded defensive. He opened the door of the van, then looked over at me. "Coming?" His tone was deliberately casual, but I got the feeling he wanted me to come along, so I nodded, trying to look as non-judgmental as possible.

I stood back a pace while he knocked on the cottage door. Next to the single step was a recycling bin, with more than a few empty beer and vodka bottles mixed with the soup cans.

No one was answering, so finally he put his hand on the doorknob and turned. The door was unlocked.

He opened it, stepped inside, glanced around, then disappeared through a doorway to another room. I waited where I was, but I could see into the small kitchen, and could make out the main decor—early greenhouse. Plants. All over the counter, cuttings rooting in glasses of water, things in clay pots of all sizes, dried stuff, weedy looking things tacked upside down on the molding near the ceiling, and baskets of hanging stuff in macrame jute holders.

"Carey, you here?" Theo called loudly from somewhere in the house.

"Yes, I'm here." Carey's voice came from behind me, and I spun around. "Hi, Boog. Great day, huh?"

She was standing near the stone wall that separated the property from the one next door. She had on baggy blue jean overalls with muddy knees, an old T-shirt with sleeves rolled up to her shoulders, and ancient sneakers with no laces. Sticking out of her pocket was a pair of dirty gardening gloves. She looked different than usual, and I tried to put my finger on it.

The sun was behind her, shining through her hair so it looked like a halo. That was it—no hat. I don't know if that was the reason, but it was as if I was seeing the real her for the first time, no masks, no shields, and I suddenly knew why Theo was hooked. My personal thermostat shot up a few degrees without warning and I felt my heart do a few heavy duty thumps. What the hell is this, I thought and retreated a step to pull my pulse back under control.

"Carey!" Theo bounded out the doorway just then.

"Checking up on me?" she asked, her tone teasing. She held out her arms, and Theo dove for them and kissed her. I had no idea their thing had intensified so much. I looked away, took a minute to detach myself from the weird reaction that had snuck up on me, then cleared my throat.

"Ahem."

They disengaged.

"Why'd you skip school today?" Theo asked. "I was worried you were sick or something."

"Nope. I just didn't feel like dealing with current events gloom and doom on such a beautiful day. I've been over helping my neighbors. I saw the van drive up. Come on over and meet them." She took Theo's hand and dipped her head at me. "You'll love them—they're vestiges of bygone days. Living remembrances of things past."

I was about to shake my head and take off, but Carey linked one arm in Theo's and the other in mine and started walking us toward the wall, chattering away as free and easy as a magpie.

"I've spent all day digging up Mrs. Benson's dahlias. She has a beautiful garden. She says it's always one of the highlights of the garden club's fall tour."

"So why are you digging it up?" Theo asked. All the worry was gone. He was his regular mellow self again. He hopped up on the wall and pulled Carey up beside him. They started stepping from stone to stone like kids. I thought again about leaving, but Carey turned and waited for me to join them, so I climbed up and followed.

"Dahlias are cold tender," Carey explained. "They have to be dug up and stored over the winter, then replanted. Mrs. Benson's arthritis has been acting up, so when I saw her out there this morning, I went over."

She jumped off the wall and headed toward the house, an old, old farmhouse, where an old, old man was sitting on the top of a rickety stepladder, set in the bushes beside a screened porch. As we got close, Carey held her hand out in warning for us to stop.

"Mr. Benson's pretty hard of hearing. I don't want to startle him," she said. I could see her point. The ladder looked wobbly enough to go, given one wrong move. He was wearing overalls, a cotton shirt with most of the plaid faded out of it, and a tattered straw hat. His head was the shape of a light bulb, with a huge forehead and sunken cheeks. In one liver-spotted hand, he held a small square of screen mesh. He was pulling wire threads off the edge of it, like a kindergartner shredding the fringe for a miniature potholder. We waited until he sensed our presence.

"Hi, Mr. Benson," Carey said loudly, reaching out to steady the ladder, which started swaying like a wooden belly dancer as Mr. Benson stood, then sat again. "These are my friends, Theo and Boog."

His lips started moving, but no sounds came out, and he bobbed his head in greeting. Then he grinned, and it was like the filament inside the bulb got a surge of juice. His gray eyes lit up and he gave a little wave of his hand, then bobbed his head again so hard, his hat slid off. Theo grabbed it from the bushes and put a steadying hand on the other side of the ladder.

"Looks good," Carey shouted, pointing to the screening behind Mr. Benson, which was patched with about a dozen neat squares. "No more flies." She bobbed her head, and Mr. Benson kept on bobbing his and before I knew it, Theo and I were bobbing, too, like a foursome of those little painted papier mâché dolls, with huge heads perched on spring necks. Carefully, Carey let go of the ladder and stepped back. Theo followed suit. We waved and left him to his chore.

"Is he going to be okay?" Theo asked. The three of us looked back over our shoulders at the same time and winced in unison, as Mr. Benson started climbing the ladder to put his patch in place.

"Well, he's been okay for ninety-three years," Carey said. "I can't stand to watch, though. Come on, Mrs. Benson's over at the vegetable stand."

Carey led us over to a ramshackle wooden lean-to type thing, that I guessed Mr. Benson had made himself. I'd actually noticed it before, driving by over the years, but just as part of the scenery. All of Yardley Hills was farmland back in the old days when the town was first settled. There are still a few working farms scattered in between the pricey real estate parcels, but more of the so-called farms are owned by CEO corporate types who play the gentleman squire on weekends.

There weren't a lot of vegetables on the rough wooden counter, some tomatoes, a few zucchinis and green peppers, a pile of onions, and some carrots. Seated on a wooden chair under the shade of the shack's roof was a woman so old her wrinkled skin was transparent, like those little envelopes stamps come in. She had on a worn print dress and a brown knitted shawl. Perched on her head was a straw coolie hat, with a scarf poked through the brim and tied under her chin. But when she looked up at us through her round wire-framed glasses, her watery blue eyes said, "I'm all here."

"Hello," she chirped.

"Mrs. Benson, I'd like you to meet my friend Theo that I was telling you about."

Immediately Mrs. Benson rose and extended her hand. She barely came up to Theo's chest.

"How do you do, Theo?" she said formally.

Then she turned to me and waited for Carey to introduce us.

"And this is Boog Buglioni," Carey said. She wasn't talking loud, so I guess Mrs. Benson's hearing was okay.

Mrs. Benson didn't even blink at the nickname. "How do you do, Boog?" She shook my hand. Hers was cool, dry, and felt so fragile that shaking it was a little scary. She stood there smiling wordlessly, her wispy little eyebrows raised as if waiting for a conversational cue from Carey.

"Theo and Boog are musicians," Carey told her.

"Oh? Now, isn't that lovely. Do you know, I kept company with a young man who was a musician, while I was attending university—I went to Boston University, you know. My musician played the oboe. Such a somber instrument, the oboe. It suited him, though, he was a somber fellow. I quite wanted to play an instrument myself. The harp, I thought, would be nice."

"Me, too!" Carey said. She looked delighted, like my sister does when she finds out that she and one of her friends love the same song or the same movie star. Like she was tickled pink to have something in common with Mrs. Benson.

"Such celestial sounds," Mrs. Benson was going on. Her gnarled fingers plucked at the air, and I had to bite my cheeks to keep from smiling at this tiny ancient woman playing air harp the way I play air guitar sometimes.

"So why didn't you learn?" Carey asked.

"Well, harps were quite expensive, and my parents were very frugal. I was fortunate they allowed me to attend university, not many young women did back then, you know. I trained to be a teacher, but then I married Nathaniel and there was so much work with the farm that I never—" Her eyes looked beyond us for a moment, then she gave her head a little shake. "Farm work doesn't pamper one's hands, and the harp wouldn't have been very practical. Still, it is one of my regrets. I love music. It rounds out the soul. I do think I'll take it up in the next life. 'Music is the language spoken by angels.' Mr. Longfellow said that, I believe. Well, I don't expect many more customers this afternoon. I think I'll close up shop and go finish the dahlias."

"I finished them," Carey told her. "All packed in sawdust, tucked in for the winter."

"You finished that whole bed? Well, you *are* a dear girl." Mrs. Benson took a moment to beam at Carey, and Carey seemed to drink in the approval like she was parched for it.

Carey helped her load the vegetables carefully into a basket. Then Mrs. Benson opened an old metal cash-box, counted out seven dollars and sixty cents and put the money in her pocket. We walked back to the house together.

"Where is Nathaniel?" Mrs. Benson murmured, a trace of concern in her voice. I scanned the horizon and pointed. He was making his way slowly to the barn, dragging the ladder.

"Now Nathaniel, come straight back when you've put that away," she called shrilly. "I lost him last month, you know. Thank heavens Carey found him in the woods behind the barn. It is so lovely to have a good neighbor. The previous tenants—well." She pressed her lips together and I got the feeling she was too well-bred to gossip, but would have had a mouthful to say about them, whoever they were.

"*Tsk tsk*. He's fine most of the time," she went on, and I assumed she was talking about her husband again. "The routines get so ingrained, you know. I do believe he just slipped back in time a bit. We used to pasture the cows out there, in the field behind the woods."

It turned out to be one of the most bizarre afternoons I ever spent. Theo hardly said a word, but he took it all in, like he was watching a fascinating movie. And Carey was perfect in the part of the farmer's daughter. Or granddaughter.

"Do you want me to put the dahlias down in the cellar, Mrs. Benson?" Carey asked when we reached the flagstone patio behind the house.

"Thank you, dear. That would be a big help. I don't handle stairs as well as I used to. Just down once in the morning and then up once to bed. I'll make some lemonade. You can stay for lemonade, can't you? It's my special recipe. Well, not mine, precisely. Nathaniel and I used to take a trip to Maine every summer, Mount Desert Island. Such a beautiful part of the world. Oh, how I did look forward to that, and we always went to the Jordan Pond House. Their gardens are divine. And that is where I learned the secret of superb lemonade.'' She looked round as if there might be a culinary spy in the neighborhood, then leaned forward and whispered. ''It's the sugar syrup.''

Carey handed Theo and me each a wooden box packed with bulbs and sawdust, and we all went into the kitchen. For a room as full of stuff as that kitchen was, it was as clean and neat as a hospital supply room. It looked as if the Bensons had saved every object that had ever passed through their life, but found a place for everything. I peeked through the doorway into the dining room, and it was the same thing. Packed to the rafters with completely organized clutter. Carey opened the door to the cellar and we followed her down the steep narrow steps.

Carey fished around in the air, found a string, and switched on the light, a bare bulb hanging from the ceiling by a frayed wire. Old furniture was stacked up all over, piles of newspapers lined one wall, and cardboard boxes filled almost every bit of space there was, except for a clear patch by the furnace.

''Over here,'' Carey said. We picked our way through the stuff to a workbench covered with tools.

''My mother would go nuts over some of this furniture,'' Theo said, looking around after we set the boxes down. ''They could have a heck of a tag sale. Maybe they should, if all their income is from that vegetable stand.''

Carey giggled. ''They don't need the money. They own about two hundred acres. All the riding trails? They lease those to the hunt club.''

Two hundred acres. I did the math in my head. The going rate for Yardley Hills raw land is at least a hundred grand an acre, which would make the Bensons' net worth about twenty million, minimum.

"Holy shit." Theo and I said it at the same time. Carey laughed.

"Why don't they hire someone to do things like patch the screens? Or put in a whole new screen?" Theo asked.

"That's just the way they are," Carey said. "They live their life, do their work, the way they always have. I did ask Mrs. Benson about getting some help. You know what she said? *'Il faut cultiver notre jardin.'* "

"What's that mean?" I asked. I take Spanish in school.

"It means, 'We must cultivate our garden.' It's Voltaire, from *Candide*. We must cultivate our garden. Sometimes it works. I mean, they're living proof, aren't they? I wish—" Carey stopped.

Theo'd been rooting around in the antiques. He came over to Carey then, and slipped his arms around her waist.

"You wish what?" he asked quietly.

I moseyed back upstairs.

The lemonade was great. We sat out on the patio in old-fashioned wooden-slatted chairs. Mrs. Benson chirped on at length about an assortment of topics, music, politics, the history of Yardley; her brain was as full as her house. All the while Mr. Benson just bobbed and sipped and grinned. He never said a word. He must have realized it just wasn't necessary for him to speak with Mrs. Benson around. But every once in awhile, he gave her a look of incredible affection. If

I were the sentimental type, it might have choked me up.

When the sun went down behind the tree line, Mrs. Benson rose from her chair and held out her hand to Theo, then to me.

"You must come again. You must come next September and see my dahlias. Carey, I was going through my sister's trunk and I found a dress—it's a tawny rust, it will suit your complexion beautifully. Why don't you stop over tomorrow and see if it fits."

"I will," Carey said. She hopped out of her chair, collected the glasses, and ran them inside.

"My sister, God rest her soul, was like Carey, like a willow, so graceful," Mrs. Benson said confidentially while Carey was gone. "Oh, I was envious, to my shame, but it seemed so much more advantageous to be taller. Most of my family, the Potters, were. But not I."

Finally Mr. Benson spoke. His voice creaked, probably from lack of use. "You're just right, Cornelia."

As Carey came back out, he stood, held out his arm to his wife, and the two of them tottered inside together.

We strolled slowly back to Carey's. When we got there, a pickup truck with the logo "Meltzer's Nurseries" painted on it was parked next to the van. The back door to the little house was open and someone was singing inside. Carey looked at us nervously.

"Well, thanks for dropping by. I'll see you." She started to hurry toward the door, as if she wanted to go in before the singer came out. She didn't make it.

A man I presumed was Mr. Harrigan sauntered out the door. He was dressed in worn khaki slacks and a gray sweatshirt, and looked pretty much like a regular guy. His hair was thinning in front, and he wore scholarly looking tortoiseshell glasses.

"Hi, sweetheart. How was your day?" He was slurring his words a tiny bit, but he seemed to be in a jovial frame of mind. He put an arm around Carey, and she went stiff.

"Hello, Theo. Hello, young man. Come in. Please, come in. Nice to have some company. Nice for Carey to have some friends."

Carey tried to smile at us, but it was as if the muscles in her face couldn't quite hold up the corners of her mouth.

"See, honey, just like I told you, right? They're already lining up at the door for you." Mr. Harrigan shook his head, smiling, but then the smile dropped away. "Gonna grow up and leave your old dad." He sighed, and the switch from happy to melancholy was so quick, I almost blinked.

"Do you want me to stay?" Theo asked. He was talking directly to Carey, not her father, and I got the feeling there was a question behind his question.

Carey bit her lip, shook her head, broke away from her father's hold, and ran inside.

Her father half-turned after her, then turned back to us. Now he looked confused.

Theo gave him a terse wave and headed for the van.

"It was nice, ah, meeting you," I said. He stared off at the pink clouds behind the tree line. I don't think he heard me. I got in the van, and we left.

chapter 7

HALLOWEEN WEEKEND, WE played a teen dance at Theo's church, a costume thing. They'd asked us to dress up, in keeping with the spirit of the occasion. Carey volunteered to be our costume coordinator, and she decked me out as the Lone Ranger, Keith as Bam-Bam Rubble, and Peter, Danny, and Theo as the Marx Brothers. Carey herself wasn't in costume, just her normal way of dressing, but with a red bandanna wound around her head and this swirly kind of patchwork skirt, she could have been a Gypsy fortune-teller.

It was one of those glitch gigs—little things kept going wrong. A circuit in the church hall blew during our second song, so we had to stop, pull a few plugs, and plug them in elsewhere. I broke an E and a G string, the E during a solo, so I played around it, the G while I was doing rhythm, so I stepped back and did a quick string change. Some glitch gigs, it feels like you're stumbling along the ragged edge of disaster, waiting for the whole thing to collapse. But that crowd was fun, the feeling was good, so we skated over the problems. Theo, Peter, and Danny were playing off each other with old Marx Brothers lines, and Theo had one of those Harpo bicycle horns, which he worked into the act.

Since everyone was pretty pumped up at the end of the night, after we packed our stuff into the van, we headed over to the Silver Comet diner. Danny's and Keith's girlfriends came, too, so we snagged two booths, making enough noise to prompt the waitress to come over and request that we keep it down to a dull roar.

I was filling Keith and Theo in on some phone calls I'd made about the possibility of a new demo tape.

"There's a guy in Newbridge Pop knows. He has a small studio, but he's good. For seventeen hundred dollars we get eight hours in the studio, with engineer and producer, a master tape, and three hundred cassettes with a cover; if we design it ourselves, it won't cost extra."

"How long will it take us to put the money together?" Keith wanted to know.

I did the math in my head.

"Figure end of February, unless we have any major equipment breakdowns. We have Valentine's Day at Eastfield Country Club. Maybe the gig at the Factory if it pans out. Those are both decent bucks."

"Is that a definite?" Theo asked.

"Not yet. I brought one of our old tapes over, and the guy liked it. He said it's down to us and some reggae band."

The Factory was a gig I'd been working hard to get. It was a real club down by the harbor that show-cased a lot of top-named local talent, older bands than us, because of the liquor license. But they'd recently started a deal where they had all age nights; they split the club into two halves, using colored hospital-type wristbands for under twenty-ones and over twenty-ones. As long as all our parents signed waivers, we could work there.

Danny turned around from the next booth. "Come up with any originals yet?" he asked Theo. "We should get them on deck, play them out a few times to polish them before we record."

"That one I told you about, the twelve-bar blues I've been fooling with, 'Elevator Man.' " He started singing right there:

> *I'm your elevator man, baby,*
> *We're goin' straight to the top*
> *Step up, step in my express car*
> *Ain't no stoppin'.*

He stopped. "That's as far as I've gotten."

"That's only eight bars," said Keith.

Theo frowned. "I know. I—"

Just then, Carey sang out spontaneously:

> *I'll take you up so fast*
> *Your ears are gonna pop.*

We all cracked up.

"If I have to tell you kids once more, you're outta here," the waitress warned.

Theo nodded solemnly, then as soon as she turned

84

around, he honked the Harpo horn at her. She spun on her rubber-soled heel and glared.

Putting his hands palms up in the air, Theo grinned his most ingratiating grin. The waitress rolled her eyes, but one corner of her mouth bent up into a smile. She shook her head and went toward the kitchen.

"I've got another one, just an idea I'm playing with. Magic after midnight, or midnight magic. The moon. I don't know. I brainstorm and come up with some phrases, bits of tune, but it's tough to put it together."

"Midnight magic?" Carey said. She sipped her coffee, then set it down, and slowly stirred it with her spoon. "Hmmm . . . midnight . . . moon . . ."

"Full moon," Theo said. "Full . . . feel . . ."

"Feel the pull," Carey came back.

It was interesting watching them—like watching two brains overlap.

Theo crunched a strip of bacon, then reached over, and slid some quarters into the jukebox on the wall. Carey put her hand over his before he could pick a song.

"No, wait. I want to think for a minute, okay?"

Theo shrugged, nodded, and went for a slice of toast, while Carey tugged a paper napkin from the silver dispenser, pulled a pen out of the side pocket of her knapsack, and hunched over the table. I dug into my western omelet. By the time the waitress came to clear the remains of the grease feast away, Carey'd gone through four napkins, each one scribbled over, but a little neater than the one before it, from what I could see.

Hesitantly, she slid the last one in front of Theo.

As he read it, I could see the excitement sweep over his face.

"How'd you do that? How'd you put that together so fast?"

"I don't know." She shrugged, but looked really pleased. "You know, magic and midnight and the moon—and then it's Halloween, and that made me think of the black cat, and—"

"Yeah. This is—yeah! Whadaya think, Boog?" He pushed the napkin under my nose, and I scanned the lines, two verses.

> *Midnight magic, moon is full*
> *Feel it tugging, feel the pull*
> *Tide is turning, flowing in*
> *Wonder what it's gonna bring*
>
> *A black cat's prowling in the moonlight*
> *Is it gonna cross your path tonight?*
> *Midnight magic in the air*
> *The wind is howling "Take care—Beware."*

I was actually fairly impressed with the tightness of it—the metaphor hung together, the images were good. And it wasn't too complicated—people would get it on one hearing. But it didn't seem finished. And I wasn't sure I wanted to encourage the collaboration. Some kind of resistance had sprung up in me. Blues Thing had always been a unit unto ourselves, musically. Theo writing original material was one thing. Bringing Carey into the process was another. For starters, would she expect to get paid?

Carey was looking at me nervously, trying to gauge my reaction. I kept it low key.

"It's not bad. But it's short—not a whole song really. And I'm not sure it's the kind of stuff we do. Not real bluesy, you know? It's—you know—I mean it might be good for Halloween, but that's only once a year, and—" I was kind of babbling, and I knew it.

Carey's eyes dropped, and she slouched back in the corner.

"I think we could work with it." Theo gave me a funny look, like he was taking it personally.

Danny leaned over from the other booth, held out his hand. "Let me see."

Without a word, Theo handed him the napkin. He read it, then hummed a few bars of a simple bass line. "Maybe some kind of swamp rock thing, like that spooky bayou groove the Neville Brothers do sometimes—I think it could work."

"We don't have a horn section." I said. "Or keyboards. How can we sound like the Neville Brothers?"

Now Theo was staring at me and it was like we'd both declared camps—opposing ones. "We do our own arrangement, Boog, like we've done for tons of songs." There was something else going on beneath the surface of the conversation and I couldn't quite figure it out, but I knew it was originating with me.

I shrugged. "Fine. Whatever. I don't care."

Theo put his arm around Carey, and carefully tucked the napkin into one of the pockets of his Harpo trenchcoat. All of a sudden I was ticked off with myself. I felt mean. Especially after all the work she'd done putting together costumes for us.

We paid up and left. I was giving both Theo and

Carey a lift, and the ride up to Yardley Hills was pretty uncomfortable. In fact, no one said a word. There were no lights on when I pulled up to the little house. Theo opened the van door, got out, and held out a hand to Carey to help her down. I had to do something to redeem myself for being such a shit heel about her lyrics. I caught her by the cape.

"Hey, Carey."

She looked over her shoulder and waited, while I floundered for an explanation.

"I'm just not—well, a highly experimental person. By nature. But work on it. Maybe come up with another verse and a bridge or chorus. We'll give it a shot."

The smile she gave me was like an engraved thank-you note. "Okay. I will."

The next day I slept in till early afternoon. I'd been going over to Anchor House to give Charlie lessons every Sunday. He'd mellowed out some, for him, but he was still a tough nut to crack, and I wasn't up for sparring that day. So I called and left a message that I couldn't make it and I'd see him next week.

Theo and Carey came over about 4:00, and we hung out in the garage. We were fooling around with a melody for "Midnight Magic."

After a short while, my mother opened the breeze-way door.

"James, you have a visitor," she said neutrally.

She stepped back, and Charlie stepped forward. His chin was out. My brain took a minute to complete the necessary synapses. Charlie was at my house.

"What are you doing here?" I blurted out. I was

fairly pissed off. The kid had invaded my territory, barged into my regular life. What did he want from me?

A little flicker of uncertainty showed in his eyes, but he blinked it away and stuck his chin out further. He balled his hands into fists and shoved them in his pockets.

"They said you were too tired to come. So I figured I'd save you the trip," he said coolly.

"How'd you get here?"

"I beamed over. Whadaya think, ya moron? I took a bus." He was rocking back and forth in his high tops. I heard the phone ringing in the kitchen, and my mother excused herself, shooting me one of her blanket warning looks, meaning, "Don't do anything you or I or anyone else will regret." Carey took it in too. She got up off the couch and stepped over to the doorway.

"Come on in. Are you Charlie?"

Charlie didn't move, but he nodded warily.

"Boog was telling us about you." That was true. "He said he can't believe how good you've gotten in such a short time. He said you're going to be a monster guitar player if you keep it up." That was a total fabrication. I swear, there were times when Carey Harrigan made Pinocchio look like the Pope on truth serum.

But Charlie's eyes lit up, and his jaw relaxed a tad. "Yeah?" he said.

"James, telephone," my mother called out from the kitchen.

Carey put her hand around the neck of my guitar,

which I was still holding. "Come on, show us what you're learning, Charlie."

Now I'm very particular about my guitars, territorial you might call it, or just plain selfish. I just don't like other people playing them. I mean, if B. B. King or Clapton were to drop by, that would be fine. I'd have no problem with either of them picking up my 355 or my Strat. They wouldn't even have to ask me. Carey gave a little tug, and I gripped the neck tighter.

"What—" I started to say.

"Phone!" Mom called again.

While I was distracted, Carey pulled the guitar out of my hand, gave it to Charlie, and started to lead him over to the couch.

"James!" The summons was urgent now.

I snorted and left.

It was Mac. "I'm sorry to bother you, James, but Charlie—"

"He's here," I said shortly.

There was a pause at the other end of the line.

"This is kind of a delicate situation. It's strictly against the rules—he's technically AWOL. But the fact that he went straight to you is very encouraging to me."

I sighed. Now I knew I was really over my head. There didn't seem to be anything else to do but start swimming. Or at least tread water.

"It's okay, Mac. He can hang out for a while."

Mom was making signals at me, pointing toward the garage, and bringing her hand up to her mouth. I tried to ignore her. She started poking me and mouthing words, like I could lip read. But I knew what she was getting at.

"Listen, my mother wants to know if he can stay for dinner."

Mom smiled and nodded. Then she poked me again and started steering an invisible car.

I rolled my eyes. "And I'll give him a ride home after."

The smile in Mac's voice sounded as broad as the one on Mom's face looked.

"I think that would really be great for Charlie. It would mean a lot to him."

I said good-bye, hung up, and went back out to the garage, where Charlie was strumming out a slow twelve-bar blues in A, his favorite key. Theo was improvising, singing along:

Sometimes you just got to get away.
I mean, sometimes, there's no way you can stay.
So you hop a bus from Newbridge
You're on your way today.

I waited till they finished.

Charlie looked at me.

"Keep practicing. You've got a ways to go," I said.

He grinned.

"So how'd you know where I live?" I asked.

"Ever hear of a thing called a phone book?" he said.

I pretended to be mad, but I wasn't really anymore. Still, someone had to keep the kid in line, and since he'd picked me—

"You ever hear of a thing called privacy? At least call first next time, wouldya?"

His grin got wider, ear to ear.

I gave up. I got out my acoustic and let Charlie keep playing the Gibson. He was getting a big kick out of playing through the amp.

We'd been out there about an hour when Allie popped through the door, dressed in her soccer uniform, sweaty and grungy as she ever gets.

"We won, eleven to three," she announced. "Mom says—"

Then she spotted Charlie. He spotted her too.

"*Aaagh!*" she shrieked, covering her face with her hands. She did an about face and slammed the door behind her. We could all hear her screaming from the kitchen.

"Why didn't you Tell me there's a Guy out there?"

Carey and Theo stayed for dinner, too, beef stew, nothing fancy, but plenty of it. Allie was late coming to the table. She made her entrance casually, showered, made-up like a model, her hair up in some girl hair things. She was wearing the forbidden jeans and a low cut shirt I suspected, from my mother's expression, would be a topic for discussion later that evening. She made a big show of sashaying around the kitchen, clearing the table after dinner. Charlie's eyes tracked every move she made.

I had to chuckle. The way I figured it, this would be Mom's payback for being such a buttinski.

chapter

8

MONDAY, SECOND WEEK in November, we got our tests back from the unit on the origins of conflict. Half objective, half essay. One essay, worth fifty points, so if you blew it, you blew the whole grade. "Discuss the origins of conflict. Give specific examples." It seemed pretty basic to me—you have human beings, you have conflict.

Theo was out with the flu that day. I spotted Carey in the cafeteria, sitting by herself, thanks to Natalie's social guerrilla warfare, so I went over. She was writing in the ever-present notebook, which she closed when I pulled up a chair.

"How'd you do on the test?" she asked.

"A minus. Seven points off on the essay." I took a bite of chicken patty on a hard roll. "You?"

"I got an I," she said.

"I thought F was the worst you could do."

She smiled and nibbled a bite of salad. "Incomplete. I'm shocked actually. I threw some more Yeats.

at her. Look at this." She folded her blue book open to the essay and handed it to me.

Things fall apart; the center cannot hold;
Mere anarchy is loosed upon the world,
The blood-dimmed tide is loosed, and everywhere
The ceremony of innocence is drowned;
The best lack all conviction, while the worst
Are full of passionate intensity.

At the bottom of the page, Brockmeyer had scrawled in tight red pen script: "Incomplete answer. Second and last chance. Lines 1 & 2 of poem—Discuss in terms of the dissolution of the former Soviet Union. Lines 3 & 4—Discuss in terms of three post WWII civil conflicts in developing nations—including the effect of modern war technology on civilian populations. Lines 5 & 6—Choose two current heads of state, one elected, one dictator—compare and contrast their power and their policies in the light of this quote. Due Friday. H. B."

I grinned. Brockmeyer really took me by surprise now and then. "She's calling you out. You gonna take the bait?"

Carey tilted her head and smiled. "Maybe."

I looked at the cover of the beat-up notebook. Not for the first time, I wondered what she was always writing in it. I pointed.

"You mind if I ask—is that like a diary?"

She patted it. "It's an everything book. Sometimes diary, sometimes things I copy out of other books. Or stuff I'm working on, you know, poems." She smiled again, kind of mischievously. "I was working on something that came into my head last night at dinner—your mom's stew.''

"Stew?" I said. "You were writing a poem about stew?"

"Hey, Boog, everything is fodder for the artist." She grinned. "But no, not a poem. More lyrics." She bit her lip and seemed to hesitate for a second. "Want to see?" she asked nonchalantly.

I shrugged a deliberately casual shrug; actually, the idea of peering into *The Life of Carey ? Harrigan* suddenly made me feel weird, almost nervous, like it would be getting too close for comfort. I guess I was afraid what I might see. But it seemed that to reject her offer would be cruel, would be rejecting her.

"Sure," I said.

She opened to the most recent page and shoved it over in front of me, and to my relief, no deep dark secrets leapt off the page. The lines were scratched out and written over, like a work-in-progress, but neatly. I read the title, "Blues Stew," and the first line, and laughed out loud.

She pretended to be offended, but I could tell she was pleased by my reaction.

"Hey, this is the blues, don't laugh. It's a sad song."

I read on.

> *I'm cookin' up a blues stew*
> *Cuz I got you on my mind*
> *I'm cookin' up a blues stew, baby*
> *Cuz you're leavin' me behind*
> *My heart's in sad confusion*
> *How can you be so unkind?*

I got a cup o' lonely
I got a pound o' pain
I need a spoon o' mercy
Say you'll come on back again.

I'm stirrin' for you, sugar
But it's a bitter, bitter brew
Without your sweet, sweet lovin'
Ain't no more that I can do
'Cept simmer in my misery
And get used to livin' on blues stew.

I wasn't laughing by the time I got to the end. In my head, I could imagine someone like Bonnie Raitt or Bessie Smith singing the words. I looked at Carey. She was coloring in her thumbnail with her pen, not looking at me.

"Carey." I closed the notebook.

"Yeah?"

"This is good. I mean, really good."

"You think?" she said, peering at me from under the brim of her gold suede baseball cap.

"Yeah, I think. You show it to Theo?"

She shook her head. "Uh-uh. I just wrote it. But I kind of wanted to run it by you first, anyway. Theo likes everything I write. You're tougher." She smiled.

"It's great," I said, and I meant it. "I wish we could use it for the band. But—you know—it's kind of—I mean—it should be a female vocal—"

"It's okay, Boog," she said quickly. "Honest. I'm just glad you like it."

I stared at her for a minute, and she stared back, questioningly, as if she was wondering what I was thinking. What I was thinking was if she could whip off lyrics like that during a lunchbreak, she probably had some serious talent. I was wondering what her other writing was like. And I was wondering if she was ever going to do anything with it, or be like that poet, Emily Dickinson, who got famous after she died, but kept her poems on scraps of paper in her drawers while she was alive.

The warning bell rang, and spared me having to explain why I'd been looking at her that way.

"Gotta go." I stood up, and started to walk away, then looked back over my shoulder. "Hey—make me a copy of that, wouldya?"

She gave me the okay sign and smiled.

Ice route, that Saturday, my turn to drive. It was a blustery day, squalls coming through one after another, when the windshield wipers couldn't keep up with the downpour, and lots of wet leaves, even more treacherous than snow for skidding. I was taking it slow, and after about two hours, my eyes were getting tired with the strain of trying to see the road through the rain. But at least I was spared the rabid ravings of the Headhunter, who only worked weekdays.

To cut out about seven miles of winding back roads, I snuck on the parkway, from which commercial vehicles and trucks are prohibited, heading over to North Newbridge.

"Hey, Boog, pull in the pit stop so I can grab a Coke, wouldya?" Theo said as we chugged up the hill toward the rest area.

"If a cop sees us, we'll get tagged," I said. But there wasn't a lot of traffic, so I pulled off the parkway and up alongside the little brick house that held the restrooms, gas station office, and vending machines.

"Make it quick, all right?" I said.

Theo jumped out, jogged inside, and was back a second later.

"Machine's busted. I'm gonna run over to the other side. Be right back."

He trotted toward the parkway, gave a quick look for traffic, did a dash to the grassy median strip that separates northbound from southbound, hopped over the knee-high steel divider, checked for traffic again, then sprinted into the other rest stop building, identical to the one on our side. I kept my eyes open for state troopers, but none of the smokies seemed to be around.

Theo was back in a flash, and he sat sipping his Coke while I navigated toward our next destination. He'd been quiet all morning, and it seemed like he was mentally chewing on something or other.

"Did Natalie call you?" he asked out of the blue.

"Uh-uh. Why?"

"Figures." He shook his head, seeming kind of disgusted.

"What figures?" I needed more data for the calculations.

"We're gonna have to do her party," he said glumly.

"No way," I said. She'd asked me at school about a week before, if Blues Thing would play the huge blowout her parents were throwing for her seventeenth birthday. From the way she described it, it sounded like it was going to be a real extravaganza, to the tune of big bucks. But a pretty nasty side to Natalie had emerged with the whole Carey and her father business, and my feeling was, I didn't really think I could put my heart into a celebration for Natalie. I'd checked it with Theo, and we'd both agreed it was one gig we could afford to skip.

"Her mother called my mother. Begged."

I stopped, right in the middle of Route 132, and just looked at him.

"Theo, I don't like her. You can't stand her. Can't you explain to your mother—"

"I tried. It's no use. Personal favor, her father and the doctor are colleagues, it would be bad politics. I couldn't say no."

I eased back into gear, totally ticked off. I hate having my life tweaked around because someone else has her own agenda. But I didn't want to give Theo a hard time for something that was out of his control. Well, maybe not out of his control, but Theo being Theo, I could see where if his mother asked him as a special favor, it would be really hard for him to say no.

"It's up to you," I said. "You want to, go ahead and tell your mother to tell her yes. But jack up the price a couple of hundred bucks. Natalie tax."

He kind of laughed, then blew out a sigh.

"What?" I asked.

"I was just thinking. You know, one thing that might be good about going away to college would be not having the 'rents butting into my private business."

"Yeah," I said. I knew what he meant, even though my parents didn't really do that kind of thing to me. "You send in any applications yet?" I asked. We hadn't talked about the college thing much, because Theo seemed to want to avoid thinking about it.

He nodded kind of glumly. "The doctor sat me down with a stack of catalogs, and applications. I sent one in to B.U. They have this communications program. I like communicating. That might not be too bad. He wants me to apply at least three other places."

He sounded so unexcited, I really felt bad for him. Applying to college, much less going, was a lot of work if you weren't into what you were doing.

"You looking at other schools in Boston?" I asked. I was thinking that would be great, the two of us up there. I already knew I wanted to go to Berklee. My interview was set up for the first week in December, but I wasn't too worried about that or the audition, which I'd heard was mostly for placement in classes. Even though my sight reading wasn't so hot, it was adequate, and I was a good ear player. With my grades being decent, I wasn't really sweating getting in.

"Yeah, I guess." He shrugged.

"Well, you have plenty of schools to choose from," I said. I tried to sound encouraging.

"You're lucky your parents are letting you be who you want to be," he said. "The doctor—" He stopped, and just shook his head.

"Can't your mother talk to him? She's always encouraged you with your music."

"Yeah, but it's different now. It's like she's waiting for me to outgrow this phase. And the doctor—

forget it. I can't even mention it without him going into a seizure. He thinks being a musician's about on a par with being a mass murderer.'' He looked over at me, then added quick, ''Not your father or anything. I mean—''

''Don't worry about it.'' I waved off the explanation. It wasn't necessary. ''Look at it this way. If you're in Boston, maybe we can get something going. It won't be Blues Thing, but it'll be Some Thing. You can still do music.''

''Yeah.'' Theo nodded. ''That's true. I don't know how it's all going to pan out.'' He gnawed on his thumbnail, which was bitten down to the quick. ''And then, there's Carey.''

''Is she making plans?''

''That's a whole 'nother can of worms.'' He stuck both hands in his hair and did a quick stir. ''How the hell did everything get so complicated all of a sudden?''

''I think it's called life,'' I said, and downshifted to take a sloping curve. ''And when you mix in love, forget it. You're just asking for trouble.''

He grinned kind of wryly at that, then sighed, leaned over, and turned up the radio.

We all went up to the Stewarts' barn late Saturday afternoon to set up, then left to take a dinner break, because we weren't scheduled to start playing till eight. When we got back, we had to park about a quarter of a mile away from the house, because of all the cars. Natalie's guest list included about half the senior class. One person it didn't include was Carey Harrigan.

But Theo wanted her to come. Carey had argued mildly against it, but he was insistent, so she gave in. I could understand the loyalty meaning a lot to her, but still, it seemed like a potentially provocative move. I talked to her about it while Theo was changing his clothes.

"Are you sure you want to go through with this?"

Carey opened her eyes wide. "Theo wants me to. He says it'll be okay."

"Yeah, well Theo tends to be a little overly optimistic about people sometimes. I'm not sure it's such a hot idea."

At that, Carey stuck out her chin a little, just like Charlie, like my saying something had made her dig in her heels, when she hadn't been sure before.

"Theo says it's fine," she repeated.

I shrugged. I'd tried. I took myself out of the loop. "It's up to you," I said.

Inside the barn, Carey parked herself behind one of our speakers and sat there, very demure, on a milk crate, and I thought for a while maybe things would be okay. Natalie hadn't paid us much attention when we came in; she was busy doing the mingle thing. When she spotted Carey, I could see the storm warnings and knew a big blow was about to rise. She marched over, dragging that poor guy from Clifton.

"Who let you in here?" She spat the words out.

Carey froze, like a deer who's just heard the click of a trigger being cocked.

Theo set his mike in the stand and stepped over, putting himself between them.

"Carey's with me, Natalie. You have a problem with that?"

Natalie folded her arms. What's the old saying, Hell hath no fury like a woman scorned?

"As a matter of fact, I do. She wasn't invited. I don't want her here."

Allan was mumbling at her, moving in front of her.

"Geez, Natalie, give her a break, wouldya?"

"Hey Natalie, come on. Let's just play some music. It's a party—let's party," Keith called over, trying to defuse the hostile tension of the situation.

Natalie sidestepped both guys, glared at Carey, aimed both barrels, and shot off her mouth. "Leave. Now." The report of the blast hung in the air.

Carey looked like she was having trouble breathing. Without a word, she sprang up and was out the side door. Theo was one step behind her.

"Throw the stereo on for a minute, or something," I said to the guy Allan. I took off after them.

Carey was running toward the head of the driveway. Theo sprinted after her and caught up with her near the wrought iron fence, and practically tackled her. He was trying to hang on, but she was just as determined to get away.

"Let me go. Let me go." I couldn't see Carey's face, but I knew she was crying. I walked over and stood a few paces away. It felt like the taco I'd had for dinner was doing a Mexican hat dance in my gut.

"Carey, I'm really sorry about this. Natalie's a blue ribbon bitch," I said.

As Theo looked over at me for a split second, Carey broke away and took off down the road.

"*Carey*!" Theo shouted. "*Damn it, don't run away like that*!" He started to dart after her, then turned back to me, and hurled a breathless suggestion.

"Go do a few instrumentals—I gotta make sure she's okay."

"Theo, wait! You can't just leave—we've got a gig! What the hell are you doing?"

He looked totally torn, but he bolted after her. "I'll be right back," he yelled over his shoulder.

"Hurry it up!" I shouted after him. What else could I do? But as I headed back to the barn, I started getting more and more peeved about the whole situation, which the two of them had practically begged to happen.

Theo never came back. Professionally speaking, the night was a disaster. I tried to fill in on a few vocals. The crowd seemed to agree with Charlie's assessment of my singing ability. They stopped short of chucking rotten tomatoes at us, but maybe that's only because there weren't any handy.

I was in my room fooling around with my acoustic after dinner the next night when Theo came over. His parents had called around 9:00 that morning, looking for him because he hadn't come home. My mother'd woken me up, saying Mrs. Stone wanted to know if Theo had slept over one of the guys' houses. Half asleep, I'd mumbled that he'd left the party with Carey. Later when I came downstairs, Mom had cornered me in the kitchen, wanting the straight scoop. "Ingrid said Natalie's mother called and told her the band ruined the whole evening. What on earth happened?" I'd winced, and grunted that I didn't feel like talking about it. The recollection was still too raw.

Theo was alone when he came, which was good, because the more I'd thought about it, the madder I'd gotten about the whole fiasco. At that moment, I wasn't prepared to extend a friendly welcome to Carey, after what her presence had precipitated.

Theo threw himself onto my beanbag chair. He looked terrible. There were dark circles under his eyes like he hadn't slept in days, and he was still wearing the same ripped jeans, and the ''Fighting for peace is like making love for virginity'' T-shirt he'd had on the night before.

''You look like shit,'' I said. ''What'd you do, sleep in the marsh?''

He shook his head. ''No, not in the marsh. I slept at Carey's. Her old man never came home.''

I raised an eyebrow, but didn't ask the obvious question about what he meant by ''slept.''

He leaned back and closed his eyes. ''Sorry I ran out on you, Boog.''

''Yeah, me too,'' I said. ''Mrs. Stewart stiffed us—wouldn't cut us a check. Said we breached our agreement.''

He didn't open his eyes. ''I know. She called my mother again. Who wasn't exactly delighted with me anyway, for coming in at noon today. Good thing the doctor was out of town. Listen, I'll pay you guys back.''

''That's not the point.'' I was getting really steamed. He hadn't been there. He hadn't made a total idiot of himself in front of a hundred and fifty kids he had to go to school with for the rest of the year. ''If it gets around that we're not reliable, we'll lose work. And especially if it gets around that I'll be subbing for you on vocals.''

Now he opened one eye.

"You didn't," he said.

"Who else was gonna?"

"You sang?" Real quick, he wiped his hand across his mouth, like he was smothering a smile.

"Yeah, I sang. If you can call it that. Get the picture? Blues Thing is us. Without you, we're Blues Nothing. We need you. So whatever's going on with Carey, keep it out of this, all right?"

The smile dropped off his face.

"Look, that's really none of your business, okay?"

"Hey, it's my business when it starts interfering with our business. I'm the business manager, remember? If you're going to screw up like that, maybe we should just can the band now." I didn't mean to say that, but I was so ticked off it just kind of blurted itself out.

Theo looked more stunned than if I'd actually popped him one. "You don't get it, Boog. Nobody gets it. I'll see you later."

He got up and walked out.

chapter

9

NEITHER THEO NOR Carey was in school the next day. That night, after we'd waited for him in the garage for twenty minutes, Theo called and left a message with my mother that he had a sore throat and wouldn't be at practice. Danny, Keith, and Peter were pissed. I was more than that, I was worried too. I told them about my conversation with Theo the afternoon before. None of us had any bright ideas on what to do or say. We decided to leave it alone for a day or two.

Tuesday, Theo was back in school, but there were already rumors buzzing through the school gossip mill that Blues Thing might be splitting up. And I was wondering myself if they might not turn out to be true. That whole day whenever we were in class together, Theo just avoided meeting my eyes. He wasn't issuing any denials.

I was home late that afternoon, in my room, fooling around with the 355, completely uninspired. Scale forms in five positions, up and down the neck, fingers moving but mind unengaged. I wasn't consciously thinking about the rift, but it was underneath everything, siphoning off my energy. Every once in awhile, it would creep up to the surface of my brain, and just kind of lie there. Then my fingers would stop moving. I was in one of those motionless vegetative lulls when the phone rang. It was Carey.

"Boog, could you come over my house at six-thirty?"

No explanation, just the question.

"I'm busy," I told her. "I have to clean my bird-cage."

"Please come. Six-thirty." That's all she said. She hung up.

I stood there staring at the receiver, listening to the drone of the dial tone. Right, I thought, very likely. You screw up my band by turning my lead singer, not to mention best friend, into a miserable, lovesick shadow of his former self, and you want me to trot up to your house for a nice chat? I don't think so.

I went back to my room, and one of those inner dialogues started up, when all your different inclinations and motivations start verbally duking it out in your head, while you yourself hang around waiting to see what the decision will be.

Theo wants to can Blues Thing over a woman? Fine, there are other singers.

Don't be an idiot. How many singers like Theo are there around who want to be in a high school band?

So what's your problem, anyway? Theo's in love. Cut the poor slob some slack.

Fine, I'll cut him some slack, but not if he screws up like that again.

I finally sorted it out to this: My pride was still

108

stinging from making a fool of myself at Natalie's party. But if it had been my girlfriend Natalie had publicly dismantled, I would have done something too. Maybe Carey came with a lot of problematic baggage. But there was something special about her. Then it occurred to me that maybe, in a way, I was chomping on some sour grapes because I was single, celibate, and, admit it, lonely. I didn't have someone. Someone pretty and interesting and with a sweet personality—someone like Carey, for instance. And that thought pulled me up real short. All of a sudden, I felt like I owed both of them an apology.

So I went. Theo's Saab was in the driveway, but Mr. Harrigan's work truck was nowhere in evidence. I knocked on the door and Carey opened it. I'd started taking note of all her hats. Tonight it was a floppy Dopey the dwarf-type knit ski hat.

"Good. You're here." She pulled me inside by the arm.

Theo was leaning against the counter, and he looked very surprised to see me.

"Hey." He said it kind of warily, and I saw him glance at Carey for a clue as to my presence.

I tossed it out quick. "Look. I'm sorry. Okay?"

He scoped me out for a long moment, then nodded. Carey was digging in the refrigerator, pulling stuff out, and sticking it inside her knapsack.

"Everybody ready?" she asked when she was done.

"Ready for what?" Theo and I asked together.

Carey didn't answer the question. "Boog, do you have gas in the van?"

"Half a tank." I gave up trying to figure out what was what.

"Good. Let's go." She picked up the knapsack and a rolled-up sleeping bag and headed out the door.

I looked at Theo. He shrugged, but grinned and I knew we were back on our old wavelength. Things were okay again.

"Where to?" I asked, starting up the van after we were loaded in. Theo and Carey were seat belted together into the passenger seat.

"Devil's Hollow," Carey said happily. Nobody said anything else for about five minutes, then I had to ask.

"Why?"

"For a picnic."

Well, naturally. Stupid of me not to have guessed. I didn't want to be the one to rain on this parade, but I felt obligated to mention that it happened to be the first day of December, generally considered winter, not picnic season, and it was about thirty-five degrees out, probably colder up at the Hollow, and we'd likely freeze our asses off.

"No, we won't. That's why I brought the sleeping bag. It's a double, and we can unzip it. We'll be fine."

So we went to Devil's Hollow for a picnic. Once we got north of the parkway, there wasn't a soul on the road. We rounded the reservoir and turned off on the road to the Hollow. The dam sluices were open and a powerful flood of water was sheeting over the concrete. The moon hung above the pine and hemlock tree line like a big old paper lantern.

"Full moon," Carey said softly.

"I guess that explains everything," I said.

I pulled the van over and parked, and we got out. From the road, we could hear the faint roar of the falls. We stepped over the post-and-wire guardrail, and stumbled over tree roots and stones, down the trail through the scrub maples and pine trees, then up the rocks, our breath coming out in little smoky puffs. The surface of the stone was moist, cold, and slippery with moss and lichen. We went all the way up to the top of the most behemoth boulder, Devil's Ledge.

Devil's Ledge is over the deepest pool. When the water's low and slow enough for swimming, the leap's about fifty feet. You have to jump out, not straight down, or you'll wind up splattered all over the rocks below. The diving pool is plenty deep even at low water, but there's one treacherous spot, where a submerged rock is. You have to know just where to aim, or you're courting death.

While Carey unloaded the knapsack, and Theo unrolled the sleeping bag, I stood and sucked in deep breaths of the cold air, that fresh running water smell, like clean dirt, or like some kind of eau de wet leaves perfume. Theo came over to stand next to me for a minute. He stuck his arm out, pointing at the wall of water-eroded rocks on the other side of the gorge, grayish-green in the moonlight, all creased and wrinkled.

"Looks like a herd of giant petrified elephants' butts, doesn't it?" He had to talk loud to be heard over the water. I cracked up.

"You're a real poet, Theo," I said.

He shook his head. "Not me. She is, though." He jerked his head back toward Carey.

Carey had spread the picnic out on the rock a ways

back from the edge. She motioned us over and the three of us sat huddled under the sleeping bag. Carey had brought the whole works—cheese and crackers, fruit, a long French bread sandwich cut into sections, napkins, even a candle. She handed us pieces of the sandwich. Theo chomped right into his.

I sniffed it. "What is it?" I asked.

"It's pâté, shallots, and cornichons," she told me.

I took a bite. It was all right. "Liverwurst, onions, and pickles."

Carey laughed. "You need to read some poetry. Boog. Listen. . . ."

I stopped chewing and listened. The water. All I could hear was the water.

> To and fro we leap
> And chase the frothy bubbles
> While the world is full of troubles
> And is anxious in its sleep.
> Come away, O human child . . .

Carey recited the words just loud enough to be heard over the flow. Something about them fit perfectly. We had the Hollow totally to ourselves. It felt like we had the whole world to ourselves. Above, the stars were sparkling like ice crystals and the sky was the deepest blue you can get before you hit black. It looked closer than usual. Way up on Devil's Ledge, it felt like we were suspended from heaven.

There was no audible music. But sitting there, looking up at the sky, I felt like we were swimming in it, the source of music, the real thing. In a way, it made me think more of Pop's jazz than what I played—

music that stretches further, reaches out, subtler, less earthy, than the blues.

"The music of the spheres," Carey said, startling me. It was like she'd read my mind. "It's all so perfect. Planets in their orbits, constellations, galaxies. Like it's all orchestrated."

"Math. Physics. Ratios. It's all numbers, Pop says."

"It's relationships," Carey corrected me. "Numbers are just descriptions. The relationships are the thing."

"The thing," Theo said. "See why I love this woman, Boog? She knows about the thing." He snugged the sleeping bag closer around her shoulders and kissed her hat.

We sat staring at the water for a long moment, then Carey zinged one out of nowhere. "I was four when my mother died."

Theo's eyes met mine, and I could tell this was the first time he was hearing this.

"How?" Theo asked softly.

"Drowned. Boating accident. My parents had a catamaran. I always used to love bouncing on the middle part, like a trampoline." She paused, then added softly, "I don't think my father ever forgave himself."

"Were you there?" Theo asked.

Carey nodded.

"Do you remember?"

Now she shook her head, frowning a little. "It's hard to explain. I remember that I used to remember—but it's like, second hand, you know? Same with my mother . . . I only remember remembering her."

We were all quiet for a minute, then Carey spoke up again.

"You know what I could never understand? I could never understand why her guardian angel didn't save her. Do you think there really are guardian angels?"

"I don't know," Theo said. "I think there's a lot more out there than we have a clue to. Could be guardian angels."

"What good are they then, if they let their person die?"

"Well," Theo said slowly. "Maybe guardian angels are like camp counselors. Maybe they each have a whole troop of humans they're in charge of. And if they're off saving one, they might miss another."

The conversation reminded me of that old Jimmy Stewart movie, with a deal where whenever a bell rings, it means another angel has gotten his wings. Like a merit badge.

"What was the angel's name in *It's A Wonderful Life*?" I asked.

"Clarence," Theo and Carey chimed in unison.

We were all quiet for a minute, looking up at that incredible sky.

Then Carey turned to us, looking so sad it kind of brought a lump to my throat.

"Do you suppose if there are angels out there, they give a shit about anything that happens down here? I mean, do they care? You think they're ever up there in that heavenly choir singing, and they take a look down at all us puny little humans, at all the lousy things that go on, and feel so bad they start singing the blues?"

Theo looked at her, and even though he was smiling a little, his eyes were serious.

"I think they probably do, babe," he said softly. "I mean, look who they got up there to jam with, Freddie, Jimi, Stevie Ray. . . . How could they not?"

We stayed pretty late. Carey and Theo fell asleep in the back of the van on the way home. I woke them as gently as I could.

"After midnight, guys. I'm beat." I yawned.

Theo did a quick scan of the driveway. No pickup truck. House dark.

"I think I'll hang around," he said casually.

I wondered how long he planned to hang around. If this was going to be a replay of the night and aftermath of Natalie's birthday bash, it didn't seem like the most prudent move in the world to me. Especially with the doctor on his case so much lately.

I shrugged. "Okay. Seeya."

"Oh, Boog, speaking of midnight, I have something for you," Carey said. She dug in her pocket and pulled out two folded pieces of loose-leaf. "Copy of 'Blues Stew,' and bridge and last verse of 'Midnight Magic.' " She smiled and handed them to me, then she and Theo intertwined and walked slowly toward the door, practically welded together.

I read the lyrics when I got home, and sat there smiling.

> *In the darkness shines the light . . .*
> *Buried in coal; the diamond bright . . .*
> *In a sea of possibilities*
> *You got to tease*

The right one out—
Seize it.

Midnight magic, might be fine
A feel, a whisper, a thin line
Tap into it—Do it, do it.
It's what you make it—take it, take it.
    Oooo-ooo-oooo
The magic's in you.

10

SECOND WEEK OF December, the first blizzard of the year dumped a foot of heavy wet snow on the state and surrounding regions. It snarled the highways with fender benders, and shut down the school systems. The radio announcer on WIGG, the station my clock radio was tuned to, was advising everyone to stay off the roads, stay home, go back to bed. Sounded like a fine idea to me. But first I had to help Pop shovel out for an emergency call, people whose electric heat had crapped out. Appetite-producing work, so afterward, I fried up a few eggs, a side of sausage, and roasted some toast. Then I went back to bed.

It was one of those great deep sleeps that's like a bonus—sleep your body doesn't need, no anxiety themes, highly entertaining dreams, which given my sex life, or lack thereof as of late, were much appreciated. Sleep at its most refreshing. So Allie yanking at my blanket and blaring my radio came as a very rude awakening.

"James, it's after noon. Come on, get up. I need you."

I wrestled my covers back and tried to ignore her, but the phrase "ignoring Allie" is an oxymoron. Especially when she's on a mission.

"Come on, James. Mom said I could invite Charlie over to go tobogganing if you'll pick him up and take us to the golf course."

Had I missed something? I winked open one eye. "You and Charlie? You only met once."

"Well, we've talked on the phone."

I could feel the tug of that last dream calling me back, so I burrowed deeper under the covers.

"Allie, they're telling people to stay home. Driving's terrible," I mumbled.

She wasn't about to give up. "That was hours ago. See? It stopped." She snapped up my shade, and I pulled the pillow over my head to block out the assault of daylight.

Allie tugged it away from me and started whacking me with it. "The plows and sanders have been out. The highway'll be fine. *Puull-eease?*"

The pillow thing was really annoying, jarring my brain every time it made contact. And all the while, she kept up a running wheedle.

"Please? Please? How often do you think Charlie gets a chance to go tobogganing? Pretty please?"

"Would you leave me the hell alone?!" I finally lost it and yelled at her. "Just get out of here! I'm not going anywhere except back to sleep."

The silence in the room was so solid you would have needed a jackhammer to break through it. I finally snuck a peek.

Allie's expression was one I'd never seen before. Controlled anger mixed with real disappointment, but more at me personally, than at not being able to do what she wanted to do. It was extremely eerie—like meeting the fourteen-year-old ghost of my mother's righteous Doppelganger.

"Ex-Cuse me," she said. "I must have been con-Fused. For a minute, I mistook you for someone who Gives a Shit."

She turned and left the room. I braced myself for the slam of a door. She surprised me again, didn't even touch it.

I groaned. Nothing like a large dose of guilt to kill a good nap.

I got dressed, not bothering to shower or shave, and trudged downstairs. Allie was sitting at the kitchen table reading a book. She didn't look up when I came in the room. I opened the refrigerator, took out a half-full quart of orange juice, and swigged half of the half. If she was trying to make me feel like a lazy, slimy, egocentric son of a bitch, she was doing a good job.

"So go ahead, already. Call him." I stood back and waited for squeals of appreciation. None were forth-coming. She didn't even blink.

"So, go on," I said. "Give Charlie a buzz. I'll go get him, and play chauffeur for you guys."

"Don't Put Yourself Out." She clipped each word.

I hate begging someone to let me do them a favor.

"Hey, I made the offer. Going once, going twice. . . ." I waited.

Allie still didn't crack. She looked at me seriously.

"You know what your problem is?"

I rolled my eyes. "I suppose you're going to tell me."

"Your problem is that you are so afraid of putting yourself out, like—like you're going to lose something. And you are going to wind up old, and crabby, and alone, and probably fat, too!" She glared at me, but the last crack made me feel like at least we were on a level playing field again.

"What are you, some kind of oracle?" I stared back at her, trying not to let her see how much her comments bothered me.

"It doesn't take an oracle, Big Brother."

"Look, I see the kid once a week, give him guitar lessons, which, by the way, I could charge twenty bucks an hour for. What are you all over my case for?"

"You see? You see?" She was so mad she had tears in her eyes.

"See what?" I was bewildered.

"You called Charlie the kid!" She slammed her book shut. "The Kid, like he could be Any kid. Sure, you go over there, Once a week, Real Big Deal, as long as it's not inconvenient for you. You're giving him a little of your time, but you're not giving him any of—of—You."

Now I was really pissed off.

"Hey, I offered. I don't have to stand here and be berated. . . . Gone." I was in the doorway when Allie launched a truth grenade at my back.

"I bet Theo would do it. And I bet He'd do it without making Charlie feel like a Beggar, either."

I clenched my teeth together, balled up my fists,

and then gave up. What can you do when someone is right and you know it?

I picked up the phone and dialed the Stones' house. "Theo, what are you up to? Listen, I'm gonna go pick up Charlie and we're going up to the golf course. Allie too. You and Carey want to come? Okay, I'll give you a ring when we get back here." I hung up, then glared at Allie. "There, you satisfied?"

Now she smiled. "Yep."

When I got back from fetching Charlie from Anchor House, Theo was waiting with Allie in the kitchen.

"New plan," he said. "Let's go up to Carey's. There's a great hill behind the Bensons' house, and we'll have it all to ourselves."

The ride up to Yardley Hills was like a backward bobsled run. Snow was banked high on the roadside. Even though the plows had been through, the road itself was slick, but there wasn't a lot of traffic, and the van took it pretty well, thanks to two new tires.

It actually turned out to be a blast of an afternoon. The hill behind the Bensons' was long and steep, bottoming out near a tiny brook that we could hear, but not see under the snow. All five of us packed on the toboggan over and over, shrieking like maniacs as we whizzed past the pines. As I watched Charlie let Allie kill him in a snowball fight, when I knew he could have slaughtered her, I was really glad she'd stuck to her guns.

He had gloves and a hat when I picked him up, but his coat was kind of flimsy for winter sports, so Carey had run inside and come out with an old parka and a scarf. I'd waited for him to fling a macho refusal at her. Instead, he stood there and let her wind the scarf around his neck, and tuck it in the coat. Grinning, no less.

By the time we'd had enough, it was getting close to sundown, and my fingers were so cold, I felt like I was gonna need a blowtorch to warm them up. We made one last run, then trudged back up the hill, cutting across the Bensons' backyard. Charlie was pulling Allie on the toboggan, and Theo and Carey were kind of propping each other up. The only sound was the crunching of our footsteps through the snow, until the clanging of a cowbell pulled us all up short. It was Mrs. Benson, hailing us from her back door.

"Cocoa anyone?" she warbled. "Steaming hot. My secret recipe."

We altered course in unison and made a sloppy parade toward the door.

"We're all wet, Mrs. B., we'll drip all over your floor," Carey said.

"Why else did God make linoleum? Now come right in, all of you. Get those wet things off. Nathaniel, help spread them out, please." Mrs. Benson clucked away all objections and waved us through.

We stayed for about an hour and a half, with Mrs. Benson orchestrating the conversation like a talk-show host. She was an encyclopedia of information. Even more than that, she seemed to sense when someone was drifting toward the edge of the conversation, and she scooped him or her right back into the middle with a remark.

By the time we left, it was dark. We climbed back over the wall to Carey's house, just as a pair of headlights cut a wavering path up the driveway. Fast. Slipping and skidding from side to side. As the lights careened around the little rotary with the fountain, I could see it was the Meltzer's Nurseries truck. One final skid across the plowed driveway, and it came to rest with the front fender snugged but good into a snowbank, just off the corner of the cottage.

We were all kind of holding our breath, except Carey, who'd taken a step back. The door of the truck opened, and Mr. Harrigan got out and stepped down, kind of listing to one side. He looked at all of us standing there staring at him and gave his head a little shake, as if he was trying to pull himself together.

"Slick. Very slick. You kids go anywhere, be careful, right?" He nodded, mostly to himself, because none of us answered. "Right. Treacherous." Then he made his way unsteadily into the house. I winced when I heard a thump, like he'd tripped over something.

Theo had his fists clenched, looking pissed-off, but helpless at the same time. Carey was frozen like an ice sculpture. Allie was squirming in her boots, looking at the ground. Charlie spoke first.

He took a deep breath, went over to Carey, unwinding the scarf as he walked. Then he took off the jacket. He draped both of them over her left arm.

"Hey, Carey this was great. Thanks, hunh?" His arm was swinging a little. After a second, he reached out, grabbed Carey's mittened hand, and shook it. "Good ta see ya again." He started to turn away, head down, then turned back, and patted her awkwardly on the shoulder. "Don't worry about—" he jerked his head toward the house—"I mean, you're you." He shrugged as if it was self-explanatory.

It melted Carey. She threw her arms around him, gave him a bear hug, then kissed him on the cheek.

"Thanks a lot, Charlie," she said, her voice kind of catching in her throat.

Allie, Charlie, and I headed back to the van with the toboggan, to give Theo and Carey a chance to say good-bye.

Charlie was grinning again.

I looked down at him and he looked at me and winked. I shook my head, and gave him a slight body check, just to keep him in line. He bumped me right back.

11

CHRISTMAS WAS ON a Friday. The Sunday before, Charlie acted kind of funny when I showed up for his lesson. We were working on some standard rock riffs, just so he'd have some tricks up his sleeve that he could show off to his friends.

"Takes a long time, hunh?" he said out of the blue.

I wasn't sure he meant learning to play the guitar; seemed like there might be something else he had on his mind. But with Charlie, I tried never to step over the line, probe, without an explicit invitation.

"This? Learning guitar?" I said.

"Yeah." He paused. "This."

"Yep," I said. "But you don't have to figure it all out at once. Just take it song by song. Or even note by note. Break it down as far as you have to till you figure it out, and go from there."

He nodded. We got back to what we were doing, but I could see something was distracting him. Usually, he focused like a pair of Swiss binoculars, putting all his stubbornness into attacking the strings.

That day, he was stopping, scanning the room, his eyes drifting toward the window, like there was something out there, beyond the walls of the shelter.

"What's the deal, Charlie?" I finally said. "Things on your mind?"

"I guess." He paused. "I guess I might not be seeing you anymore."

"Why's that?" I asked. I sat back in my chair and stared at him.

"I'm going back home. My mother finally kicked the bum out. For good." He spoke casually, but I picked up this guarded joy his mask couldn't quite cover.

"That's great, Charlie. But what do you mean we won't be getting together? I can come to your house, no big deal. You're doing great, but you have a long way to go—"

He was shaking his head. "It wouldn't work. I've got a lot of stuff to do and all. Help with the kids, and—"

I looked at him. He looked back for a second, then down at his sneakers.

"Well, that's great," I repeated. "That you're going home." I didn't know what else to say. "I'm really happy for you," I added. And I meant it. I was glad for him. But at the same time, I felt a little twinge of something that surprised the hell out of me. As if when I'd decided to do this, I'd moved some things around inside myself to make room for Charlie, in spite of myself. I'd kind of gotten used to him occupying this certain spot in my life. And this particular spot was going to be empty without him in it. As close as I could call it, I was going to miss the kid.

"Well, you can keep practicing anyhow," I said.

He shook his head. "This isn't my guitar. I can't take it with me."

He looked at the Martin, and all of a sudden, his mood went into a tailspin. He lifted the guitar like he was getting ready to hurl it, but then he stopped himself at the last second, laid it gently on the couch next to me, and bolted from the room.

I think I know how he felt. I don't like good-byes either.

Every year, the Stones throw a big Christmas eve bash, an open house. It's been a tradition ever since they moved in. Neighbors come, relatives, colleagues of Dr. Stone, all the kids' friends. Mrs. Stone always has the house decorated like something off the cover of a holiday magazine. The whole nine yards: massive tree, table groaning under platters of food, a bottomless punch bowl of spiked eggnog, Christmas carols. Big-time good cheer.

I was up in my room getting dressed to go. But something was bothering me. My guitars were in their cases, lined up on the floor next to my desk. One of them was an old beat-up acoustic I always used when I went to the beach, or picnics, any place where I didn't want to have to worry if someone else picked it up to fool around, or if it got a few dings. Another was my Guild D40C.

I'd gone through a lot of guitars over the years, trying, buying, selling. It's just a feel you get when you find the right guitar, it fits you. The 355 was one. The Guild was another.

It didn't seem right that Charlie had to give up the

guitar when he left Anchor House. The idea had passed through my mind a few times that week to try and dig him up a guitar of his own, but I hadn't done anything about it. But as I stood there with my sweater half over my head, all of a sudden, it became an urgent matter. I knew I wasn't going to be able to get into any kind of Christmas spirit if I didn't do something about it.

I went down to the den to get wrapping paper, scissors, ribbon, and tape, brought it up to my room and started to truss up the case with the hack-around guitar, after tucking an extra set of strings inside, and a little note saying "Merry Christmas."

Then out of nowhere, this voice popped into my head: *That's big of you, Boog, giving Charlie the beat-up guitar.*

I ignored it, and kept wrapping.

Give him the Guild, the voice whispered.

I sat on the bed next to the half-wrapped hack-around case, and thought about how many acoustics I'd gone through before I found this guitar. And about the five or six big ones I'd have to shell out to replace it, assuming I could even find another one in this good shape. And about the hundreds—thousands maybe—of hours of playing time I'd invested in it.

The voice said one more thing: *Forget it, Boog. You don't owe Charlie anything.*

"Shit," I said out loud. I shook my head, grabbed the Guild, and headed downstairs, before I could change my mind.

The clincher was, maybe I didn't owe Charlie anything, but it seemed like someone, something did. And I had this feeling that whoever or whatever owed

Charlie was trying to work through me at that moment, weird as that might sound. If I blocked that effort, it was going to haunt me.

Mom was in the kitchen putting the finishing touch on a plate of smoked salmon hors d'oeuvres she always brings to the Stones' party.

"You're bringing your guitar?"

I shook my head. "You guys go on ahead. I'll be over a little later."

She gave me a questioning look, but didn't say anything else. I grabbed the van keys from the hook by the door, put on my coat, and left.

As I left the house, it was just beginning to snow, those first few stray flakes. I got on I-95, the most direct route into Newbridge. The trip was quick. The roads were fine, and there wasn't much traffic. Newbridge is only five miles away, but it could be a light-year from Yardley, it has such a different feel.

I got off the throughway and headed toward the waterfront. The scattered holiday decorations seemed pathetic in the rundown neighborhoods I drove through. Like they were saying, "Merry Christmas? Happy New Year? Who are you trying to kid? Every new year is worse than the last. Peace on Earth? In a city with one of the worst homicide rates in the northeast? Good will? Yeah, we know all about it. The used clothing bins, with castoffs from you guys who have everything."

But Anchor House stood out again, warmed the chill the drive through the city had settled on me. It was all lit up, and there was a wreath on the door. Through the window, I could see the Christmas tree and a ton of people. Some kind of party going on.

There was a guy at the gate, all bundled up, and he came over to check me out as I pulled up to the driveway.

"Hi. Can I help you?" He shuffled back and forth on his feet and rubbed his gloves together.

"I have a present for one of the kids. Charlie Elliot. Do you know him?"

The guy nodded. "Charlie went home yesterday. But go on in. Mac's inside."

He unlocked the gate, and I drove through. The small parking lot was jammed. He motioned me over onto the grass.

"Just leave your keys in case we have to do some rearranging," he told me as I climbed out of the driver's seat.

I went around front and rang the doorbell. I almost fell over when Miss Brockmeyer opened the door. She was wearing a fluffy dress, high heels, and makeup. Not a trace of military stiffness in her manner. She looked just as surprised to see me as I was to see her, and it seemed to take her a second to place me in this different context.

"James, come in. Mac didn't mention you were coming tonight."

"He didn't know," I said, stepping through the door. "I didn't know."

Pine garlands were scalloped all along the edges of the wood molding. Some fancy choir recording of "Deck the Halls with Boughs of Holly" was weaving through the white noise of dozens of different conversations. It was almost like a holiday gathering the house had originally been built to hold.

"There's a coat rack in the office," Miss Brock-

130

meyer said. Then she added, "You know Charlie went home yesterday?"

I nodded. "I heard. I can't stay, anyway. But I brought him something. A present."

She looked down and took in the guitar case, and suddenly her eyes got bright. The smile she gave me was just like the kind my mother always did, when I was a kid and brought home some over-pasted grungy valentine or Mother's Day thing I'd made in school.

I took a deep breath, handed her the guitar, almost had to force myself to overcome a tug of resistance.

"I'll make sure that he gets it tomorrow," she said. "Merry Christmas, James." She looked like she was thinking about maybe hugging me, and that was something I really couldn't have handled, so I took a step back toward the door, fumbled behind me for the knob, gave her a little wave, and took off.

As I stood on the front porch, it sank in that my Guild was gone. But somehow, instead of an empty feeling, what I felt was this lightness. It's funny. I've learned not to expect instant gratification for efforts I've made; playing the guitar tends to teach you that. But that feeling was so strong, so tangible, it was like I'd gotten a wink from God. Like he wanted to let me know, *You did the right thing, Boog*.

On the way back, the snow was coming down thicker and starting to stick. Everybody was taking their time on the throughway, as if no one wanted to mar the serenity of the evening with even a slight fender bender. I didn't have the radio on. But I was sensing music—silent music or music on some frequency I wasn't perceptive enough to hear yet. Like the night at Devil's Hollow.

131

I was part of this harmony, is the best explanation I can come up with. The tires were humming, the wipers swiping back and forth, that provided a background rhythm. Then there were the snowflakes hitting the windshield, like feathery noiseless drumbeats, polyrhythms, so complex you don't get them at first, the pattern's too sophisticated. But then something clicked, and for a few seconds, I was plugged in, I got it all, perfectly in tune with something so big, so grand all I could do was float in it.

It was crowded at the Stones', noisy, boisterous with joy, the kind of confusion my mother calls "happy hubbub." Ice cubes tinkling in glasses, chatter punctuated by laughter, shrieks of little kids racing around, getting way out of line because the grown-ups are all too mellow to stifle them. And music. Some kind of medieval sounding instrumental stuff, with a lot of horns. It was like a canvas and the party was being painted over it. From somewhere in the house, Theo's room no doubt, I detected the pulse of a bass keeping solid time. It could have been total chaos, cacophony, except something was pulling it all together.

I stood in the front hall for a minute, mapping out a strategy. *Refreshments first,* I thought. As I spotted my parents across the living room and waved, Mrs. Stone came up next to me.

"Merry Christmas, Boog." She kissed me on the cheek. "Food's in the dining room, help yourself. The gang's upstairs on the third floor." Then she glided off to perform some other hostessly duty.

I threaded my way through the crowd, stepped over a few rug rats who were playing a game of crawl tag between the forest of legs, and procured a roast beef sandwich with horseradish sauce from the massive spread of edibles on the dining room table. I got a Coke from the bartender to put out the fire from the horseradish sauce. Then I just stood and watched all the good cheer flow for a bit.

I was watching Theo's mother. She worked the crowd like a master mingler. Making sure people had drink refills, drifting from group to group chatting, stooping to move a little kid away from the fireplace. Every time the front door opened, she was on the spot greeting the guests. It hit me that night, how much she and Theo were alike—they both had tons of energy and they both came across like the whole world's friend. And it was genuine—it was just a function of their never focusing only on themselves, but always projecting themselves out to other people.

A few stuffed mushrooms, a miniature quiche, and some crackers and a chunk of cheese log later, I was ready to make my move. I cut through to the kitchen where the caterers were keeping up their end of the party and went up the back stairs to Theo's room, following the sound of the music, Stevie Ray and Double Trouble.

I stood in the doorway for a second, plotting my course into the crowded small room. Carey was there, sitting real quietly on the floor at the foot of the bunkbed, half hidden by the closet door which was open. Her hat, a red Jed Clampett number, was askew. Theo's sister Ellen, home from college, was sitting on the bottom bunk with some guy I didn't know, and Eric, home from London for the holidays, was fooling around with Theo's computer. A few cousins, junior high age, were playing poker on the floor. And Allie was stretched out next to them, trying to look suave though I could see she was on the verge of giggles, while Theo teased her, singing along to "Little Sister." He was decked out in new blue jeans and a red long underwear shirt, and in what I called his bounce-around-the-room mode, hyperenergetic.

Theo gave me a wave but didn't stop singing, and Ellen and the guy shifted over to make room for me on the bed. I picked my way through the bodies, sat down, and settled in, feeling good.

"Look at him," Ellen reached over with her stocking foot and poked Eric. "Just like when he was a baby. Remember the Jolly Jumper, Eric?"

Eric turned away from the monitor, and the two of them watched Theo, who was totally oblivious to the scrutiny.

"That's probably what did it to him. Jumping up and down in that thing all the time. Gave him a sense of rhythm." Eric shook his head and grinned. "What a scrawny kid he was. Still is."

"Stop it. He is not. Don't pick on him." Ellen whacked Eric on the shoulder.

"Hey, someone had to toughen him up. The way Mom and you girls babied him."

Ellen snorted. "You toughened him up good. Remember when you dropped him down the stairs?"

"It didn't hurt him. He just bounced. Look, he's still bouncing. I helped shape him into the man he is today."

I had to chuckle when Eric said that.

All of a sudden Theo turned around and tuned into the fact that he was the topic of conversation. His brother and sister smiled at him and he smiled back, and not to be disgustingly sentimental, it was a beautiful thing.

I looked down at Carey, and she looked back at me. Seemed like she was about as far away from a partying mood as you can get.

"Hey, Car, how's it going?" I said.

She looked up at me, and forced a small smile. "Hangin' in there, Boog."

I looked at Theo and raised my eyebrows. He gave me what seemed to be a helpless shrug, then he walked over and squatted down next to her.

"I just figured it out," he said, grinning. I could tell he was trying to jolly her up.

"What?" she asked.

"This." He wiggled her hat. "Makes me feel like you're ready to hit the road in a heartbeat. You know, like, take off your hat and stay a while." He flipped it off her head.

She smiled at him, but snatched it off the floor and jammed it back on.

About 10:30, Mrs. Stone called us all down to sing carols, another tradition, before people start taking off to go home or to midnight church services.

Carey stopped off at one of the second floor bathrooms, and I pulled Theo aside.

"She okay, Theo?"

Theo looked at the closed bathroom door, ran his fingers through his hair, and sighed.

"She was fine until the Stewarts showed up."

"Natalie was here?"

Theo shrugged, looking depressed. "What was I supposed to do? Her father's one of the doctor's buddies. They play golf together. I couldn't exactly tell my mother to tell them not to come to an open house.''

"Did Carey and Natalie have, ah, words?" I asked.

"Natalie doesn't need words." Theo looked grim when he said that.

Carey came out of the bathroom, looking like she'd splashed some water on her face, tried to liven herself up a bit. We went downstairs.

In the living room, Ellen sat down on the piano, and we went through the standards, "The First Noel," "Silent Night," "Joy to the World."

I was standing on the landing at the bottom of the stairs, so I had a broad view of the room, and everyone in it. Carey was sitting on the loveseat, staring out into space, and Theo was perched on the arm, next to her. Gradually, all the Stones kind of gravitated together. Dr. Stone had his arm around Mrs. Stone's shoulders. One of Theo's little nieces toddled over and started climbing his blue jeans. Theo hoisted her up, grinning, but still singing, totally unselfconsciously, choirboy training. I was watching Carey watch them all, and her eyes got bright.

As Ellen went into "It Came Upon a Midnight Clear," Carey suddenly jumped up off the loveseat, half-losing her balance, and bumping the end table, sending a dish of ribbon candy flying. It landed on the hearth with a crash, shattering. The smile dropped off Theo's face. Tears were streaming down Carey's cheeks, as she pushed her way toward the front door. Theo handed his niece over to his brother and started after her. As he brushed past his mother, she touched his arm. He paused to give her hand a quick pat, but his eyes were on Carey, and he rushed to follow her out the door.

chapter 12

JANUARY DRAGGED LIKE, well, January—maybe the inevitable slump after the holiday high. I slogged through the month, a dreary cycle of school, work, band practice, a few pedestrian gigs, sleep, feeling like I was half in hibernation.

February I got a slight surge of energy. It was dark as doom on Groundhog's Day; the little rodent didn't have a prayer of seeing his shadow, so I was hoping maybe an early spring would roll around. I was starting to feel restless, like I was ready to move on to something new, like a lot of what I was doing was lame duck living, biding time. Maybe that's inevitable, too, when you're a senior. Anyhow, I was getting tired of the old routines, case in point, Brockmeyer's class.

"So we have an Amazonian Indian who makes a subsistence living gathering Brazil nuts, a cattle rancher, also Brazilian, who needs cleared land to graze his cattle, an environmental group whose main focus is on preserving the rain forest, as well as another one whose primary interest is in the survival and welfare of indigenous peoples. And finally, we have an international banking concern interested in economic development, dealing with Brazilian politicians who have a variety of motives—and who argue that since it *is* their country, they have every right to dispose of its resources as they see fit.

"All right. Homework. An essay, five hundred words, the topic, 'Whose interests are the best interests and why?' Due day after tomorrow."

The class had gotten to the point where it didn't bother groaning anymore. What came out was more like a soft communal sigh of resignation.

Carey had been slouching in her seat the whole period. Now she spoke up without raising her hand, in what seemed to me to be a non sequitur.

"What difference does it make what we think? I mean, nothing's gonna change." She sounded so defeated I was taken aback.

A glint flashed in Brockmeyer's eyes that seemed as frustrated as it was angry.

"Not with an attitude like that. We're talking about use of resources. On the one hand, we have natural resources, a finite supply. On the other hand, human resources. There's certainly an abundance of waste in that category." That comment was as pointed as an ice pick. "You 'Think globally, act locally.' "

The bell rang, cutting the exchange short. Everyone stood and started the exit shuffle, everyone except for Carey, who sat staring at a spot on the bottom of the wall. Theo stepped over next to her, looking a bit perplexed, and more than a bit worried. He tugged on the brim of her Meltzer's Nurseries baseball cap. She kind of shook herself out of the trance she was in and put one of those pasted attempted smiles on her face.

Theo shook his head back at her. "Sorry, can't fool me with that. What's the matter, Car?"

Carey let the smile fall off like it was a relief not to have to put forth the effort.

She sighed quietly. "I don't know. Just down. Maybe it's me. I just don't know. Theo, can you tell me something?"

For a second he looked like he was going to make a funny comeback, try to cheer her up, then he seemed to change his mind. "I can try. What?"

"Do you think this life is some kind of test, or what? And if it is, how come it's like a little pop quiz for some people and a life-or-death outcome one-shot exam for others? Like—like—oh, like the kids of that Amazonian Indian who's scavenging nuts just to survive. Or even, like, well, someone like Charlie. Can you tell me?"

When she mentioned Charlie's name, I felt a twinge of guilt. I wondered how he liked the Guild. He hadn't sent a thank-you note or anything, not that I'd expected one, it wasn't his style, but still, I wondered. I reminded myself to remember to give him a call one of these weeks.

Theo, meanwhile, was looking thoughtful. Finally he shrugged.

"I don't know, baby." He gently tweaked a lock of her hair back away from her face. "I think sometimes it doesn't do to overthink it. You do what you can do where you see a chance to do it, and hope for the best, I guess."

Carey caught me looking at them and smiled, wryly, but a real smile this time.

"What do you think, Boog? Think this life is a test? And if it is, you suppose God grades on a curve?"

The night of the Valentine's Day Dance at Eastfield Country Club's junior clubhouse, a cold front was blowing through, no snow, no rain, a black sky with the wind howling across the fairways, arctic cold and clear. Inside it was packed enough you could feel the body heat. Carey came with us, looking pretty hot herself, dressed in a short and slinky black number, under a loose, maroon velvet jacket with beads and sequins sewn on in a big-scale paisley design, and the velvet squashed bell hat. Obviously second hand, but very effective.

Before Blues Thing started up, she and Theo took a stroll on the golf course. They'd left one of those small bottles of champagne in a snowbank behind the driving range, so I figured they were popping the cork and toasting each other. Dr. and Mrs. Stone were away for the weekend and Theo had the house to himself. Carey had brought a small overnight bag with her, which she left in the van, and I gathered that they had special plans for the evening, after the dance. They came back in with cheeks red as construction paper hearts.

First set, we cranked, no need for warmup, we just blasted right off. The crowd was fairly swanky, typical Eastfield C.C. up-and-coming generation. It was basically a couples crowd, except for one group of prep school types, in blazers and khakis, and a gaggle of girls who hung around one of the speakers ogling Theo while we played.

We finished off with a Clapton version of Robert Johnson's "Cross Road Blues," then Theo and Carey disappeared for the break again. When they came back, they were both grinning like Cheshire cats. Made me think about rethinking my term in rehab from the female gender.

We went into the second set in high gear. Sometimes when Theo cues me into a solo, I play it safe, stay in known territory with licks I can do in my sleep. Other times, usually when the crowd is just right, the energy exchange between us and them flows in a way that it's all amplified, so it flows like one big whirlpool, drawing everybody into the middle of the music together. That's when it kind of takes me over. I explore, go out on a limb, dive into a solo, and just go with it. Sometimes I wipe out, and my fingers flail back to the tried-and-true riffs I've practiced till they're surefire. But when it works, it's a rush like no other. Something in me breaks into new space and I can feel myself expanding. It was one of those sets for me.

To pace the crowd, we slowed things down with "Little Wing," classic Hendrix. Theo and Carey were into it full tilt; you could just about see the current arcing between them in the semidark room. Carey slid her jacket off and dropped it on the edge of the stage, in a kind of Salome move, then went on dancing by herself. Then we cut into Double Trouble's cover of "Come On," a real driver by Earl King, which revved things up again, and really stoked Carey's engine. By halfway through the tune, she'd danced herself to the middle of the dance floor.

I watched while one of the preppies, a tall, well-built guy with long hair pulled back in a ponytail, and so cocky he might as well have had "God's Gift to Women" tattooed across his forehead, worked his way over to Carey and started dancing next to her, kind of with her by default. She just grinned a friendly grin and kept on gyrating, but the look in the guy's eyes made me a little wary. They danced the whole rest of the set.

When we wound up, Carey smiled at the guy, said something, and turned around to make her way back toward the stage. At that moment, Theo was flanked by the flock of females. They were making requests for the next set and practically drooling on him. One of them, a tall sultry redhead, put her finger on his chest and traced the fake lapel on his tuxedo T-shirt.

My eyes shot back to Carey. She'd seen it, too, and it seemed to pull her up a little short. Ponytail was on standby. He whispered something to Carey and made a motion like tipping a shot glass into his mouth. She glanced back at Theo. Now the redhead was clinging to him like bargain brand plastic wrap, way more intense than your average run-of-the-mill groupie. I knew it didn't mean anything, but I could see it was having an effect on Carey. But the kicker was when the vamp pulled Theo's head down and kissed him full on the mouth. Carey turned away woodenly, nodded at the guy, let him put his arm around her, and lead her away. She didn't see Theo extract himself from the woman's clutches and retreat from the whole groupie brigade, back behind the drums, where he wiped his mouth with the back of his hand.

As I gave the five-minute warning for the last set, Theo scanned the room, frowning a little.

"Hey, where'd Carey go?" he asked. "Ladies' room?"

I shrugged ambiguously. I didn't want to be the bearer of ill tidings, but I had a bad feeling about it. The whole group of guys was gone.

We jumped into "Tuff Enuff," but I could tell Theo was preoccupied now. It was a fairly canned rendition. Still no Carey. A slow blues was next on the playlist. Halfway through, Carey stumbled in with Ponytail, wearing his jacket. She looked out of it, and he was smiling like a rattler who'd just consumed a mouse and still had the tail hanging out of his mouth. Carey could hardly stand up and I felt like taking the guitar string I'd just changed and garroting him with it, when I saw the effect the scene had on Theo.

As he absorbed what was going on, I could feel something drain right out of him. Then he did something he'd never done before. He turned his back on the audience and finished the song with his eyes closed.

When I got home, about 2:30, Mom and Pop were still awake, talking in the kitchen. Pop always needs some wind down time after he plays, and he had the ingredients for a super-duper, guaranteed-to-give-you-gas-and-wild-dreams sandwich spread out on the table—hoagie rolls, ham, salami, black olives, lettuce, pickles, mustard, onions, provolone, mayo.

"Want one?" he asked.

"Sure," I said.

"Jeannie?"

Mom shook her head. She was leaning against the counter, and she reached over to snap a wilted blossom off the bougainvillea, which had finally flowered.

"Carey certainly had the prescription for what ailed this plant," she said.

I grunted, scenes from the night flashing back through my head like a lousy movie. Theo was a mess when I dropped him off at the house. Alone.

Mom tuned in. "What's the matter, honey?"

Pop had finished assembling the gastronomic masterpieces. He sat across from me and slid my sandwich across the table. I chomped down and chewed, trying to figure out where I wanted to start with this, or if I wanted to start with this.

"You guys started going out when you were in high school, right?"

He nodded. "Senior year. Your mother was doing a story for the school paper on the jazz ensemble. I played her a little 'Scrapple From the Apple.' "

"I fell for his bebop." They smiled at each other, then Mom hopped back to the topic I was beginning to think it might be better to just avoid, with that intuitive aim of hers. "How *is* Carey, by the way?"

A pickle slice slid out the back of Pop's sandwich, and he caught it in midair and popped it into his mouth. I didn't answer directly, I asked another question.

"Did it interfere with you and your other friends, the relationship? Change things? Change your life? Change you?"

They both looked at me thoughtfully, like they were trying to figure out what I was really asking.

145

"You and Sharon get back together?" Pop asked.

I snorted. "No way." I took another bite. "It's not me. Theo. And Carey. How is she? Don't know. She and Theo had a major blowout tonight. She got pretty drunk with some other guy. He must have poured it down her throat, he practically carried her out."

Now Mom and Pop exchanged disturbed looks.

"You know, I wondered," Mom said slowly. "That first night Theo brought her over. The name Harrigan rang a bell. A teacher over in Clifton had been fired right about the time there was the big push to set aside funding for the student substance abuse program. I remember one nasty editorial mentioned the incident. That must have been awfully hard for Carey. . . ." Her voice trailed off. She looked at my father again, some kind of message look that I couldn't decode, but he did right away.

"Lot of drinking goes on at these things, huh?" Pop asked casually. He's no dope, and he's been around the music scene long enough to know what the climate is, with regards to mood- or mind-altering substances. I got the feeling he wanted to get a bead on where I stood on the issue at that point in time.

"Enough, I guess." I shrugged. "I stay away from it pretty much, when we're playing. Makes me too sloppy, throws my timing off."

He nodded to me, and then to Mom. They both seemed satisfied with my response.

"Well, I hope Theo works things out with Carey," Mom said quietly. "And I hope she doesn't start looking for answers to her problems in a bottle. Alcoholism often runs in families. I would think getting fired would have been enough to shake her father into doing something. Do you know if he goes to AA?''

"It doesn't look that way," I said.

After a minute, then slowly began it response. You
know it's the strength to stop only...
If you...to 5:30, you know at for next later...
...know, together, and he I said.

13

THE PHONE RANG about 3:30 the next afternoon, just about the time my system was really waking up.

"I'll get it!" Allie did a broad jump for the receiver and snatched it off the wall.

"Why don't you get it?" I suggested.

She stuck out her tongue. "Hello?"

After a second a look of disgust passed over her face. She flung out her arm, pointing the receiver at me like a weapon.

"I'm ex-Pecting a call, if you don't mind."

I didn't engage, just took the phone.

"Boog?" It was Carey's voice, sounding very hesitant and very raspy.

"Yeah?" A wall went up in my mind. I didn't think I was ready to hear whatever she had to say.

A long silence followed. I just waited. I'm good at that.

"How bad was I?" she finally asked.

I almost dropped the phone in disgust.

"You're asking me?"

Another pause, then a very hesitant response. "Yes, I'm asking you."

I bit back about five stinging retorts, and tried to keep my voice from showing how pissed I was. "Well let's put it this way, I hate seeing a guy cry. Especially when he's my best friend."

"Oh." Her voice couldn't have been smaller.

"You want to know how bad you were, you're asking the wrong person. Ask Theo. He's the one you burned."

I could feel the anger building in me. And oddly, a touch of disappointment too. I felt like she'd let me down in some weird vicarious way, by what she did to Theo. And to herself. I thought I'd better hang up before I said something I might regret.

"Listen, I gotta go."

I had the phone halfway back to the wall when I heard her call out, "No, Boog, wait. Please." Slowly I brought it back to my ear.

"What?" I said.

"I'm sorry."

What did she expect me to do, grant her absolution? Give her a medal? I shook my head.

"Would you tell Theo?" Her voice was barely a whisper. "Tell him I'm sorry and that I love him?"

"Call him and tell him yourself," I said, and hung up the phone. I stood there swearing under my breath, trying to decide if I should get involved in some kind of reconciliation. I decided not.

Carey wasn't in school on Monday. Theo was, in body, anyhow, but definitely not in spirit. I felt like I had a zombie sitting next to me at lunch.

"So, have you talked to her?" I finally asked. I thought maybe he needed to get it off his chest, vent a little.

He gave his head a slight shake, stirred his hair, closed his eyes, and shook his head again.

I wasn't sure if I should say anymore. But he looked so miserable, I figured it might be worth a shot.

"She called me yesterday."

His eyes flew open.

"Yeah? And?"

I finished the last bite of slag they call American chop suey at Yardley High. "She sounded pretty sorry, Theo." I sighed. "And she said to tell you she loves you." I almost had to force myself to say that second part, but I was glad I did, when I saw the effect on him. Like a shot of adrenaline straight to the heart. The doomed look left his eyes.

"Thanks, Boog." He stood and picked up his tray.

"You off?" I asked.

He nodded. "Think I'll make a phone call."

Wednesday after the Valentine's Day Emotional Massacre, Theo and I were doing our ice route. He and Carey had gotten back together from all appearances, which was good as far as I was concerned, because Theo down in the dumps was just not Theo. They were inseparable as Krazy Glued Lego blocks once again. And they were both wearing matching silver rings. I wasn't sure what that meant, and I didn't ask.

I was driving the truck, and we were listening to, who else, the Headhunter on WIGG.

"So, the doctor goes, 'Mr. and Mrs. Jones, I have

some good news and some bad news. The bad news is: your baby was born without a body. The good news is: you've got a beautiful, otherwise perfectly healthy head, and a colleague of mine is working on a total body transplant operation.''

"Hehcheh." Theo was already chuckling. I rolled my eyes and swung onto Route 77.

" 'So, you folks take your head home, and I'll give you a call when my buddy's got the kinks worked out of the procedure.' ''

"Seventeen years, eleven months and twenty-nine days later, the Joneses get a call from the Doc.

" 'Mrs. Jones,' he says, 'Sorry I took so long to get back to you. Listen, procedure's perfected, we're ready to roll on the transplant. Got a donor body on ice, operating room booked. So bring Head down to the hospital tomorrow.' ''

"Heheh. Hehcheh." Theo's shoulders were starting to shake.

"Mrs. Jones is ecstatic. 'Oh, Doctor,' she says. 'This is fabulous news. Tomorrow is Head's birthday. He will be *so* pleased!' She goes running up the stairs, taking them two at a time, and bursts into Head's room, shouting, 'Head! Head! We have the most wonderful birthday present for you!' ''

"Head looks at her, rolls his eyes, groans, and goes, 'Oh no! Not another hat!' ''

Theo lost it, went into hysterics. "Not another hat! Not another hat!" He was practically choking he was laughing so hard, doubled over his seat belt.

In the background, I could hear all the people at the WIGG studio laughing too. I couldn't keep from cracking half a grin.

"Coming up at the Factory, the Ultimate Battle of the Bands, round one." The Headhunter's announcement blared from the speakers over a hot drumroll. Theo pulled himself together, leaned forward, and turned up the volume, shooting me an eager glance.

"Listen, Boog."

"You want to glom more details, stay tuned to the Headhunter at WIGG ninety-five point five FM." Then he stuck on a Doors tune, "L.A. Woman," just as I pulled the truck into Wells Rest, the last stop in Littleton, the town directly north of Eastfield.

"I'll get this one." Theo hopped out and scrambled to get the freezer stocked before the song ended.

I still hadn't been able to nail down the Factory gig. The guy was giving me kind of a runaround.

The Headhunter came on again just as Theo climbed back in the truck.

"Ultimate Battle of the Bands, round one, sponsored by WIGG FM Radio and the CD Connection. Friday, March nineteenth at eight PM. Six bands will be chosen to compete, on the basis of demo tapes. Send your tapes to the Headhunter, care of WIGG radio. Round two Friday, April second. Winners of both rounds to battle it out in the Ultimate Playoff, Friday, April sixteenth."

Theo'd whipped out the small notebook he'd started carrying with him to jot down song ideas, and he was scribbling all the info.

"First prize: one thousand dollars; cash, folks, and a six-date contract at the Factory, and airplay on WIGG FM."

"Boog, we gotta get that demo made. We gotta. This is our big chance." He was like an excited electron, getting ready to bounce to the next orbit.

"That's a lot of money to spend, Theo. I don't know."

"So what? What else are we gonna do with it?"

"How about split it up at the end of the summer and use it for college?" I suggested.

"Don't talk to me about college, okay?"

I could see his stubborn streak kicking in, so I let it drop.

Who was I to piss on his corn flakes? And, truth be told, I wasn't unexcited about the idea, though I thought it was a bit of a long shot.

"Let's talk it over with the other guys on Sunday, at practice," I suggested.

"Okay, so it's decided then." Theo was grinning, happy as a clam, like he always was when he'd sold us all on one of his ideas. "Blues Thing demo. All we have to decide next is which tunes we want to do."

"We should put an original on it, don't you think?" Keith said.

I nodded. "Which one though? We don't have that much to choose from."

Theo winked at Carey, who was curled up in a corner of the old brown couch. He was smiling like he was about to pull an ace out of his sleeve. In fact, he pulled a piece of paper out of the pocket of his flannel shirt.

"I just happen to have something here," he said.

"You really think we have time to work up a new one?" Danny asked.

Theo nodded confidently. "Twelve-bar blues—

piece of cake, nothing new with the changes. Plus, that'll showcase Boog the best on the lead.''

He handed me the lyric sheet.

DREAM ENGINE
by Theo Stone and Carey Harrigan

I'm ridin' a dream engine
I'm arrivin' at your station
In my dream engine
The ultimate transportation
I'm drivin' my dream engine, baby
Get ready for your dream vacation.

Don't need no steam for my dream engine
To go where we're goin'
No slow twenty mule team, baby
Can you hear my whistle blowin'?
This is one trip you can't afford
To miss, baby, come on board.

What you see ain't what it seems
We're headin' deep into dream country
We'll ride through amber waves of brain
On the ecstasy express train.

I'm startin' up my dream engine
Don't get left behind
Chuggin' my dream engine
Through forty-eight states of mind
Fuel up your imagination
Paradise is our destination.

A little chill snaked its way through me as I read. I could hear Theo belting it out, a solo, a fresh one, played along in my mind, underneath the words. And that was just on the first read-through.

I passed the paper along to Danny. Theo was looking at me expectantly. Carey was half-hiding under her hat, but peeking to check my reaction.

I couldn't keep the grin from spreading over my face. "I like it."

Danny had passed the lyrics along to Keith.

"Theo, how come forty-eight states instead of fifty?" Keith asked.

Theo and I exchanged a glance, kind of a smile about Keith's way of looking at things, and one that said we knew exactly what the other one was thinking.

"Continental U.S.A., Keith," I answered for Theo.

"Plus it's got the internal rhyme," Carey put in.

The whole band agreed. "Dream Engine" for our debut original. I said I'd set up the recording session for next week, and we scheduled three extra practices. Grueling pace, but we were under a deadline.

When they all left, I went in to the kitchen for a soda. Allie was doing homework at the table.

"Charlie said to say hi," she told me.

I winced a little. I still hadn't gotten around to getting in touch with him. Since coming out of my January slump, I'd been busy doubling up and catching up on other stuff. I knew it wasn't any kind of excuse. And I also knew there was something else to it, some kind of inertia against getting overly involved, maybe.

"So, how's he doing?" I asked, taking a Coke from the fridge.

Allie cocked an eyebrow at me. "Why don't you Call him and Ask him?"

Heheh. A Theo chuckle, minus the amusement. More or less what I'd said to Carey about him the week before. Hearing it from Allie in reference to myself was annoying.

14

THE DEMO TAPE turned out great. We wound up putting three originals on it: "Dream Engine," "Midnight Magic," and "Blues Stew." I'd played the devil's advocate when Theo brought up that idea, said I thought it really needed a female vocalist.

"Don't let your mother or your sister hear you talking like that, Boog," he'd grinned.

"Yeah, a lot of great chefs are guys, Boog," Peter had put in.

I felt kind of sheepish and said fine, and Theo did a killer version of it, so I was glad I'd agreed in the end. The tape was good enough to earn us a slot in round one of the Battle of the Bands. Theo crowed like a rooster when I told him.

"See? The Headhunter recognizes quality. I bet most of what they got was commercial regurgitation."

We decided to practice every night in the week and a half remaining until the competition, to make our five song set tighter than a snare. Wanted to get the timing perfect, too—we'd have exactly twenty minutes to strut our stuff.

Monday, Tuesday, and Wednesday nights, energy was high, as if the challenge injected us with a dose of serious motivation. I felt like we had an excellent shot, at least to make the play-off round.

Thursday, Brockmeyer's class was the first class of the day. Carey hadn't been at band practice the night before, and she wasn't in her seat when the bell rang. Brockmeyer came in with a stack of corrected term papers and started passing them out.

We'd chosen our own topics for the papers. I'd done mine on the effect of a powerful country embargoing a small underdeveloped country in order to influence the politics. The conclusion I'd reached was this: If a powerful country further cripples the economy of an already impoverished country, the people who lose the most are the same ones who always lose—the ones without the power to make any political changes anyway.

We were supposed to propose our own solutions to the problems we picked. This was mine: Forget about the politics, forget about military aid, just bypass the goons with the muscle and go straight to the people who need the help, and give it to them. As I paged through, I could see Brockmeyer had a load of comments about the practicality of my suggestions and the ripple of effects that spreads out from any given cause. Like, if you donate tons of rice, it can actually undermine the economy even more, by making the price of rice plunge, thereby doing a number on the local rice farmers who are trying to eke out a living. "There are no easy answers," was Brockmeyer's final comment. But she gave me a B+ for content and research, and an A− for style and proper format. So I was happy.

As Brockmeyer handed out the last paper in the stack, the classroom door opened, and Carey waltzed in. Well, maybe waltz isn't the right word. It was kind of a combination of mincing and stumbling. Halfway to her seat, she caught her toe on the floor and almost pitched headlong onto Brockmeyer's desk, but she recovered and made it to her seat. She slid into it carefully, smiled at Theo, turned and smiled at me, then folded her hands in front of her.

"Where's your late pass?" Brockmeyer snapped.

Carey frowned as if the question perplexed her. She made a big show of searching through every pocket on her person, in her backpack, even checked the cuffs of her sleeves. Then she sat back and gave a helpless shrug.

"Go get a late pass," Brockmeyer said grimly, but evenly. "Don't come back without one."

Theo was leaning forward in his seat, like a runner poised on his mark, as Carey smiled a dumb smile, sighed, collected her gear, and made her way back to the door. There, she turned and waved to Theo, who half rose in his seat.

"Stay." Brockmeyer gave the command like a dog trainer, pointing at Theo. Slowly, he slumped back down. Carey shrugged again and left. She never came back, with or without a late pass.

The second the bell rang, Theo sprang for the door. I watched Ms. Brockmeyer watch him go. Whatever she was thinking made her look like she had a case of lockjaw. We had a free period next, and I went to try and find Theo, to warn him that Brockmeyer looked like she was ready to head up a posse and maybe the better part of valor would be for Carey to discreetly disappear.

Down in the hall where all the senior lockers in Winston House are, Carey was leaning against the wall. Her locker was open, and Theo was rooting through it furiously, saying something to her through clenched teeth. Carey's eyes were closed, and she was still wearing that stupid smile. From the bottom of the locker, Theo pulled out a pint of vodka, half-full. He slammed Carey's locker door closed with such a bang, everyone in the hall froze and stared at them. Carey's eyes popped open. I guess he'd finally caught her attention.

At that moment, Brockmeyer came through the fire-doors and advanced on the two of them, full-speed ahead, torpedo bays open.

She looked at Carey with fairly undisguised contempt, then at Theo, who was still holding the bottle, and a touch of something like regret crept in. Brockmeyer reached out and took it from him.

"Is this yours?" she asked Carey.

Carey closed her eyes again, and didn't answer.

"Is it yours?" She repeated her question to Theo.

He didn't say anything either, just pressed his lips together.

Brockmeyer tilted her head, and I could see she was struggling with something in her own mind. When she spoke again, her voice was calm, but it held a hint of serious warning. She stared hard at Theo, a look that seemed to say, "I'm going to give you one chance here."

"If you tell me this is not yours," she said carefully, "I'll believe you."

Theo glanced at Carey, then at me, over Brockmeyer's shoulder. I saw it all over his face—he was going to take the rap.

"I can't tell you that," he said quietly.

I waited for Carey to speak up, to come clean. She didn't.

Brockmeyer scrutinized Theo for a few seconds, then nodded in a neutral way.

"Both of you. Come with me." She turned and headed in the direction of the office. Theo took Carey's arm and started to lead her away.

First offense for possession of alcohol on school grounds: automatic three-day suspension, and a parent has to escort you back to school when the suspension's up. For Theo, not for Carey, who apparently wasn't too far gone to know when to keep her mouth shut. And Theo didn't turn her in. The policy is, if a teacher suspects you've been drinking and confronts you, and you admit it, they can suspend you. But not if you don't admit it. And not if they don't catch you red-handed. They don't administer Breathalyzer tests at Yardley, not yet, anyway. So even though Carey was crocked, they didn't kick her out, Theo told me on the phone that night, while his parents were having a conference on their wayward youngest son.

Theo was in the trough of a major depression when I stopped by his house the next day with assignments; you're on your own making up work missed when you are under suspension. Carey might as well have been suspended, because she hadn't shown up anyway.

I went up to his room, and he was lying on the top bunk, hands under his head, staring at the ceiling. Not even music on the stereo.

"So, what's the story?" I asked casually.

He sighed. "Which story do you wanna hear, Boog? The story about me being grounded for a month—oh, which includes all gigs and the Battle of the Bands, by the way—"

"Shit!" I stared at him. "You serious?"

"Or the story about Carey and her father getting sixty days notice to find a new place to live because the owners of the mansion's daughter is getting a divorce and moving back to be with Mumsy and Daddy on the ancestral estate?" he went on. "Or—"

I cut him off.

"That why Carey was drunk at school? What's the big deal? They can get another place."

Theo's shoulders twitched in a weary shrug. "Partly, I guess. That and the fact that it's probably a little tough to take when your old man's sobbing through his own slobber and asking you what you're gonna do—" The last part of his sentence, his voice got very hard, and I had the feeling that if Mr. Harrigan walked through the door right then, Theo, nonviolent as he was, would have kicked his ass into the next century.

I walked over to the desk and sat down. I wasn't mad at that point, I was more like numb. The news about the Battle of the Bands, everything we'd worked for, not to mention the seventeen *C* notes we'd spent making the demo, all of it being down the tubes, hadn't really sunk in yet.

"Can I ask you a question?" I said.

Theo didn't answer.

"I can understand you taking the rap for Carey at school, I really can. Although I have to say, I don't understand Carey letting you. I mean, if I really loved someone—"

"Think about it, Boog," he interrupted tersely. "Remember the deal with being suspended? A parent's gotta bring you back?"

"You mean, she's embarrassed to be seen with him?" I asked.

"That's part of it. I mean, he starts drinking when he wakes up a lot of days. But I think it's more—I think she feels like she has to protect him from public opinion. It would hurt her to think she was exposing him or something."

"Okay. I can buy that," I said. "But why don't you fill your parents in on what really happened? I'm sure they'd believe you. Then maybe you wouldn't be grounded and—"

Theo was already shaking his head.

"Why the hell not?" I exploded. "Your chivalry's noble and all, but you're paying a price here for something you didn't buy."

"Look—my parents don't like Carey. Natalie told her mother some stories and blamed the whole birthday party thing on her, and Mrs. Stewart passed it all along. So now my parents think Carey's bad for me, and I'm not going to give them any more ammunition, all right?"

I tried to reason with him. "Theo, there are other

things at stake here. It's a lot of money we're throwing down the crapper, backing out of the gigs we have lined up—not even counting the prize for the Battle of the Bands, which we've got a good shot of winning. And if we get that studio time—and airplay on WIGG—think, buddy, think! There's a lot to lose."

He clammed up.

I finally went so far as to resort to parent tactics, guilt specifically. "How do you think the other guys are going to feel? You're not only letting yourself down, you're letting down four other people. Supposedly your best friends. How can you do this to us?"

At that, he swung himself off the bunk abruptly, looking torn between anger and despair.

We stood there staring at each other.

"Man, it really pisses me off, her letting you do this. Anything she can't hack, she runs away from. I bet she's got it all written up in that notebook of hers." I shook my head in total disgust.

Theo's shoulders slumped, like he was too tired to try and defend her anymore, but nothing I'd said had changed how he felt. "If you can't figure it out, Boog, forget it." His voice was drained.

I left. On the way downstairs, I toyed with the idea of spilling the whole story to Mrs. Stone. But something held me back.

The other guys and I decided to cancel band practice until Theo could be there.

"I don't know, Boog," Keith said. "We're going to be splitting up at the end of the summer anyway. Maybe the time to do it is now."

I argued. "This isn't the way we want Blues Thing

to end. We owe ourselves more than that."

"What do we say when kids at school ask us what the deal is?" Peter wanted to know.

"I'm going to put a note on the mailing that goes out this week. Something like, taking a short break, working on new material, back soon, better and blue-sier than ever."

"I don't know," was Danny's comment. He played the funeral march on his bass.

"Come on, you guys. We don't want to fizzle out. Let's get through the month, I'll start lining up more gigs, we'll have a killer summer and wind it up the right way."

In the end, I talked them into it, but no one was very happy.

The phone call that Sunday night surprised the hell out of me. It was about 5:30, one of those sullen late-winter evenings, the aftermath of a sleet storm that had scoured the state. The precip had stopped, but the cloud cover stayed, old man winter at his wet-blanket worst.

I was in the kitchen, salivating at the smell of some curried chicken deal simmering on the stove, which, according to Mom, wouldn't be ready for another hour because the spices had to "meld." I had my Gibson out, not plugged in, and I was struggling through a jazz book Pop had tossed my way when he heard the band was on hold for a month.

"A break's not necessarily a bad thing, James. Use the time to do a little musical exploring on your own."

I'd taken enough lessons to know how to read music fairly well, but I'd never really explored any jazz theory. I'd just come across this interesting thing called modes. You play a major scale, your basic doe-a-deer scale, say in the key of C, no sharps, no flats. If you start the scale on the second note, go re to re, you have what's called the Dorian mode. Same notes, completely different feel—it's minor now, so it sounds sad. You keep on playing in the key of C, always those same seven notes, each time starting the scale on another note. There you've got your seven modes. All different moods, you might say—the emotional emphasis changes, the color of the music.

I picked up the phone automatically when it rang, like an answering machine.

"Boog, it's me. Can you come over right away?" It was Carey and she sounded out of breath and scared, as if she'd just finished running a half marathon with a pack of hungry wolves on her heels.

"Who's me?" I asked, even though I knew exactly who it was. I'd pretty much had it with her. Her letting Theo get suspended, not to mention grounded, was the final straw, the one that really busted my hump.

"Me, Carey. Please—" Her voice was small and almost petrified. "It's Mrs. Benson. She fell. I think she might have broken something. She can't move and she's crying—I don't know what to do."

"Why are you calling me?" I asked. I wondered if she'd called Theo first and his parents had said he couldn't go. But my brain was already racing ahead: Obviously, her old man either wasn't home or was too drunk to be of any help—what did I do with my keys?—get coat—good thing I put some gas in the van.

"I was afraid to call Theo's house. His parents have been bugging him about us being too serious. Plus, you know, the thing with school. I called you because you seem like you always know what to do." She answered both my spoken question and my unspoken one.

My whole body had gone tense, braced as a huge wave of resistance to getting involved swept over me. Then I thought of that tiny woman, lying on the floor, chirping in pain. I really didn't have a choice. Sucked in again.

"Call nine-one-one. I'll be there in ten minutes," I said.

"She doesn't want me to—she doesn't want to leave her—"

I cut her off. "Carey, do it. Call an ambulance. Don't move her. Get a blanket over her, try to keep her calm." I hung up, stuck my guitar back in the case, got my keys and coat, and headed for the door. Halfway there, it occurred to me that maybe Dr. Stone was around. In spite of Carey's reluctance, I thought it might be a good idea to call him, so I dialed Theo's house. Mrs. Stone answered and I briefed her quickly on the circumstances. She's good in a crisis, like most of the mothers I know, react and act now, collapse later.

"I'll send him right away. Theo can go, show him where the house is."

Dr. Stone's BMW was already tearing up the street by the time I was backing out of my driveway. The van can't compete with those German roadsters.

When I got to the Bensons', Theo was waiting at the back door and let me in. I couldn't read the expression on his face, a half-frown, not angry, maybe more puzzled.

We went through the kitchen into the hall, where Dr. Stone was kneeling next to Mrs. Benson, who was lying on the floor at the bottom of the stairs. Mr. Benson was sitting on a straight-back wooden chair near the front door, and Carey was standing next to him, with one hand on his shoulder.

"It's okay. Everything's going to be okay," she was saying softly.

I wasn't sure how true that was. Mrs. Benson was whimpering as Dr. Stone examined her.

"I don't want to go to the hospital," she said over and over. "I don't want to leave my home."

"Now, don't you worry." Dr. Stone's tone was authoritative, but reassuring at the same time. If he told me not to worry, I'd be inclined to do what he said. "I think you've broken your hip. You'll need to be in the hospital for a little while, to get you on the mend. But I'm sure you'll be back home in no time."

"Who'll look after Nathaniel?" The concern in her question kind of choked me up.

"Do you have any children? Any family in the area?"

"No," Mrs. Benson whispered. "We weren't blessed. Although dear Carey—" She sounded like she didn't have enough breath to talk. Dr. Stone shushed her gently, and right then the ambulance pulled in the driveway.

"Theo—" Dr. Stone barked. Theo took off like a shot to show them in.

168

It was so bad when they were loading Mrs. Benson onto the stretcher, her sobbing, her cries of pain, that I had to restrain myself physically from putting my hands over my ears. I saw Carey couldn't quite manage that. Her eyes were closed and she was pressing her palms against her ears. Mr. Benson looked shaken, helpless, and very confused.

Dr. Stone helped the EMTs get Mrs. Benson into the ambulance, then came back in for a moment.

"Mr. Benson?" he said gently. "Mr. Benson, would you—"

The old man looked at Theo's father as if he was speaking Greek.

Dr. Stone kind of sighed, then smiled, and spoke slowly. "Mr. Benson, why don't you try and get some rest? I'll have someone come by in the morning."

Mr. Benson looked blearily at Theo's father and nodded vaguely.

Dr. Stone looked at Carey, a poker face that gave no indication what he really thought of her. "Is there anyone who can come and stay with him?"

Carey cheeks flushed, and she swallowed. "I don't think so. Not that I know of. I live next door."

"How about your father? Could he organize some neighbors to look in?"

Now Carey looked at her shoes and shook her head, then looked up again. "But I can come over and stay, during the day at least. I help out a lot, I don't mind—"

His jaw stayed stern, but his eyes softened.

"What about school, young lady?"

Carey didn't answer.

Checking his watch, Dr. Stone took a step toward

the door. "I'll run up to the hospital now. I'll have someone there get in touch. Maybe visiting nurses . . . Theo, you tell your mother I'll be home in an hour and a half. You can get a ride home with Boog."

Dr. Stone left.

"You want me to stay and help?" Theo dipped his head toward Mr. Benson.

"No," Carey said slowly. "I don't want you to get in any more trouble because of me. Your parents must hate me enough as it is."

"They don't hate you." Theo's denial came back too quick to be the whole truth, I thought.

I took my keys out of my pocket and jingled them quietly, a little hint.

Carey turned her head away. Theo took hold of her chin and forced her to look at him.

"Hey, it's you and me. It's us. It doesn't matter what anybody thinks."

"I'll be in the van, Theo," I said, and made for the door.

"Why did she call you instead of me?" Theo asked, the second he got in the passenger seat.

I shrugged and started the engine, backing out of the Bensons' not very well-shovelled and bumpy with ice driveway. "I think it's just what she said, Theo. She didn't want to get you in any more trouble with your parents. She's got to know that your parents know you well enough to realize that the vodka wasn't yours."

"They're still pretty pissed. I don't see why they're making it such a huge big deal. It was only a three-day suspension."

I really felt like Theo was missing something important. If I were a parent and saw my kid getting sucked deep into the quagmire of someone else's problems, I think I'd be pretty frustrated. If his folks had put two and two together, knowing them, they were probably even more upset about him lying than about the booze. But I didn't go into that with him.

"Theo, is it really worth it? I like Carey. You know I do. But it seems like ever since you got involved with her, you've—I don't know—I mean—you used to be happy, remember? Is she really worth turning your whole life upside down for?"

"Yes." Not a dot of hesitation.

I guess you can't argue with love.

It was close to eight when I got home. I walked in on the end of a world class mother-daughter bout.

"You Do Not UnderStand!" Allie screamed and left the room.

"No, I Do Not!" Mom yelled after her. She banged open a cabinet, snatched out a dish, stomped over to the stove, yanked the lids off the two pots there, ladled me out a mound of congealed rice, doused it in curried chicken and vegetables, and put it in the microwave.

Allie, meanwhile, had shaken the plaster with a champion door slam, after which she kindly provided some dinner music by putting on a tape, metal so heavy it had to be off the periodic table of elements.

Mom took a deep breath, fished my dinner out of the microwave, put it on the table, and started doing the dishes.

"Is everything all right with Carey's neighbor?"

she asked. She had to talk pretty loud, because Allie had the music cranked up so loud the light fixture in the ceiling was actually vibrating.

I nodded.

Mom glanced up at the ceiling.

"She knows I hate that—that—black, nihilistic, life-stinks cacophony. I used to play songs for my parents to try to get them to understand my point of view. If the song itself said something. But that—" She pointed up at the ceiling with the ladle she'd just rinsed. As if sensing she was getting to Mom through the ceiling, Allie bumped the volume up a few notches. It was more than Mom could take.

She jumped up on the chair and started banging on the ceiling with her ladle. The decibel level subsided a hair or two. Sighing, Mom stepped down, and sat on the chair, letting the ladle fall to the table.

"Why don't you just tell her to turn it off?" I asked.

Mom's eyebrows did a little jig. "Since when have I ever been able to tell your sister anything? It was telling her something that started this whole brouhaha. She wanted to meet Charlie at the mall and 'hang out' and go to a movie. I said no, that he could come over here. I even offered to pick him up and drive him home."

"Oh," I said. Guilt again. Seemed like the longer I put off getting in touch with Charlie, somehow the harder it was to think about doing it.

The tape stopped for a moment, then a new one went in. If the other was toxic, this one was spewing lethally radioactive fallout.

"That's it!" Mom jumped up from her seat.

"What are you going to do?" I eyed her a tad nervously. My mother has a long fuse, but when it ignites—watch out.

"I'm going to fight fire with fire, that's what I'm going to do." She stalked out of the kitchen.

A moment later, the stereo in the living room started pumping out Bach's Brandenburg concertos loud enough to rouse old Johann Sebastian himself from the grave. In spite of being down about the whole business with Mrs. Benson, I had to chuckle.

chapter 15

BLUES THING GOT back together once Theo's parents lifted the edict, but we never really got back together, if you know what I mean. Something had changed, or was in the process of changing. Maybe it was me. I could tell after the first hour of band practice that it wasn't reversible. After spending a month digging into jazz theory on my own, our old material, our old arrangements seemed kind of restricted. I felt, well, confined might be a way to put it, musically. I wanted to experiment with some things, but the other guys didn't seemed inclined to go where I wanted to go with the music.

I guess maybe what the band had lost was cohesion and forward momentum. Practices were sloppy. I never followed through to see if we could sneak into round two of the Battle of the Bands after giving up our slot the first time or on the Factory gig either. The few gigs we did play were flat, overprocessed. Something had definitely gone stale for me. And Theo was somewhere else, not just another planet, more like whirling around the galaxy on an errant asteroid. One thing that hadn't changed though, he and Carey were a tighter unit than ever.

First half of April, rainfall came close to hitting records, and it seemed like the whole world was in a funk. More trudging through school days, work, home to watch Allie spar with Mom, with the stakes independence.

Last week in April, I finally got my acceptance to Berklee, and along with it, a surge of impatience to just jump ahead and get on with the next phase. Theo got his acceptance to Boston University that Thursday. He showed me the letter after school, when he came out to the van to catch a ride home.

The Saab had finally given up the ghost for good, so I was squiring him around a lot. A few times, I loaned him the van so he could take Carey out. When I asked him about his new car plans, and all the money he'd saved, he went vague on me, and I gathered he'd spent the money on something else. When I asked him what, he wouldn't tell me, just said he'd ordered it, and would show me when it came.

"That's great, Theo," I said, reading the letter. "So why do you look like you just got rejected from the Acme School of Basket Weaving?"

He answered with a question. "Did you know Carey's not going to graduate?"

I shook my head, but I wasn't surprised. With all the days she'd missed, she had to be flunking at least phys ed, which is enough to keep you from getting your diploma. She hadn't turned in a term paper on time, and Brockmeyer doesn't accept late work, so she was probably flunking history too.

Theo rubbed his head. "I was thinking maybe we could get an apartment together up in Boston and maybe she could finish up somehow and . . ."

"You mean live together?" I asked. "You ready for that?" I was semistunned.

He let out a long sigh. "When I mentioned it, the doctor practically ruptured his vocal cords. They won't pay my tuition unless I live in a dorm or live with them."

"What do you mean, 'Live with them'? You gonna commute three hours each way every day?" I stared at him.

He looked disconcerted, like he'd let something slip out unintentionally.

"Are you moving? Are your folks moving? To Boston?"

"Listen, Boog," he said nervously. "I wanted to wait till it was a sure thing before I—"

Now I was definitely stunned. I shook my head to get my brain started again. I mean, we'd be in the same city, going to school, most of the year anyway, assuming Theo went to BU. But still, it wouldn't be the same. That was when it hit me full force that life was really changing, and it was going to drag me along with it, ready or not.

We both saw Carey running across the lawn at the same time. Her knapsack was slung over one shoulder and her sneakers, tied together by the laces, were over the other. Theo stuffed the acceptance letter in his pocket.

"Do me a favor and don't mention it, okay?" he said hurriedly. "I haven't told—"

Carey opened the door, climbed in the van, over

Theo's lap, and crouched down in the middle between the two seats.

"Look," she ordered.

Theo did a 180 degree scan.

"At what?" I asked.

"Everything." She spread her arms out. "Look at the forsythia. Do you know, I used to make them out of sticks and yellow crepe paper in the middle of winter? And look at those trees—all those tiny baby leaves." She leaned over, rolled down my window, then rolled down Theo's. "Smell," she said. She inhaled like a connoisseur of air. "Spring. It is officially here."

"Time to do that spring thing," Theo murmured, smiling at her.

I cleared my throat so they wouldn't start up with any mushy love-bird crap.

"We have to celebrate," Carey said.

"What do you have in mind?" I asked.

"Devil's Hollow. You don't have to work today, do you?"

"No, but—" I had things to do. Things I wanted to do. Guitar things. I looked at my watch. Carey reached over, unbuckled it from my wrist, and tossed it in the back of the van.

"Step off the treadmill for an afternoon, Boog. Come on."

Theo was grinning, his dilemma apparently set aside for the moment.

It was an extraordinary day, I had to admit.

"Okay." I turned the key and went to shift into reverse, when Natalie appeared at Theo's window. She folded her arms and leaned right in.

"Hi, guys. Hey, Theo, tell your father congratulations for me."

I put it together a little too late to slap a gag over Natalie's malicious mouth.

"My dad says it's one of the most prestigious teaching hospitals in the country. And Chief of Orthopedic Surgery. Wow. Are your folks going to live right in Boston or one of the suburbs? Marblehead's gorgeous."

Theo didn't say a word. A funny smile played over his mouth as if he was having a hard time believing this stroke of bad luck, Natalie popping up just at this moment.

Carey was looking back and forth between the two of them.

"I'll be up at Wellesley. That'll be real close to you."

Natalie got in a final shot. "We'll have to get together. Well, gotta run. Bye, Boog. Bye, Carey. See you, Theo."

She stepped away from the window.

"Not if he sees you first, Natalie, I'll bet the ranch on that," I called over. She held up her hand and flipped me the bird.

I rammed the van into reverse, then looked at Carey in the rear view mirror.

She wasn't there. It was a ghost sitting next to me. Theo had his arm around her shoulders and was trying to talk to her.

"Carey, I just found out."

She spoke then, just a whisper. "I knew this was too good to last. I haven't let myself think about you going away to school. . . ." Her voice trailed off.

"But I'm not going. Listen to me." Theo put his hand on Carey's chin and turned her face, forcing her to look him in the eye. "Do you hear me? I'm not going. Or if I do, we'll find a way for you to come too."

Not sure where I was going at that point, I drove slowly. No one said anything for about ten minutes. Carey returned to her physical body from wherever she'd been as we were passing Burger King on the Post Road.

"It doesn't matter," she said quietly. Then she took a deep breath and smiled brightly at us both. "Well, let's go already. Devil's Hollow. We're wasting half the afternoon driving around."

It was eerie, like the conversation with Natalie had never happened. She was positively cheerful. A few times, Theo tried to explain, but she put her finger to his lips and shushed him.

It was a still a little early in the season, so we had the Hollow to ourselves. We hiked up to Devil's Ledge. Every few feet, Carey was off the trail, checking out some botanical specimen. Jack-in-the-pulpits. Clumps of skunk cabbage. Next to a moss-covered rock beside the small stream that bypassed the falls and trickled down from a pool, she came across a patch of small white flowers. She knelt down, her back to us, picked one, then stood up, and turned around. Her hand was covered with blood.

"Geez, what'd you do?" Theo was on her like a boy scout going for his first-aid merit badge. "Is there broken glass?"

She laughed. "Bloodroot." She shook him off,

held up the flower, squeezed the stem, and red-orange sap flowed out the bottom. "The Indians used this for all kinds of things. Dying cloth, curing skin cancer, cough medicine. They even painted themselves with it to scare their enemies away." She dabbed some on her nose.

"You're not my enemy," he said quietly.

Carey didn't answer. She took the oozing stem and dotted two lines from the outside corners of her eyes, down her cheeks. They looked like tears of blood. Then she tossed the flower on the ground and hiked on up the trail. Theo stood still for a minute before he followed.

The big rock up top was warmer than toast. Carey lay down on her stomach, chin on her arms, and watched the waterfall splash down into the pool. With all the rain we'd had, the flow was strong and loud. I stretched out on my back, and Theo stood with one foot planted on either side of Carey's hips, like a body guard.

Suddenly he stepped aside, ripped off his T-shirt, kicked off his shoes and blue jeans, and stood there in his plaid boxers. "Time to take the plunge."

He beat his chest a few times, curled his toes over the edge of the rock and dove.

I tensed, listening for the splash that meant he hadn't splattered himself all over the rocks and exhaled slowly when I heard it a second later. Chalk up another death-defying leap for Theo Stone.

"*Whoooo—eeee!*" His howl rang up, bouncing off the rocks. Carey turned back to look at me and we shared a smile.

He climbed back up, walked over to Carey, shook

his dripping body over her. "It's very refreshing." He looked at me. "You gonna go for it, Boog?"

I shook my head. The more I thought about it the harder it seemed.

Theo cocked his head at me, like he was puzzling something out. Finally he smiled. "You know Boog, I think sometimes you get in your own way."

He sat down on the rock next to Carey, and they both stretched out. I didn't want to let him see how his comment had stung me. I edged away from them a bit, stuck my hands behind my head, closed my eyes, and just lay there, absorbing the spring warmth. At one point, I heard Carey whisper.

"It's such a hopeful month, April. Everything just starting." She paused. "But it's over so quickly. Such a fragile time." She sounded sadder than I'd ever heard a girl sound.

"I won't go," Theo whispered to her.

"You have to," Carey said.

"I won't."

I could tell from the slurping noises that some spit-swapping had started. I gave them a minute, then sat up with my back to them, as noisily as I could. By the time I turned around, Theo was sitting up too. He seemed restless now, drumming his fingers on the rocks, raking his hair, which was almost dreadlocked from the swim, looking around.

"Anyone hungry?" Carey asked.

"Could be," I said.

The question seemed to provide a focus for Theo, a relief that there was something he could do.

"Hey, I'll pop over to the General Store for some sodas and sandwiches. It's only a few miles up the road." He pulled on his jeans, shirt, and socks, and stepped into his sneakers.

"Want company?" I asked, even though I didn't really feel like moving. The sun baking me was making me feel real lazy.

"Nah. I'll make the run. You guys stay and enjoy. I'll be back in half an hour."

I tossed him the keys.

The minute Theo was out of sight, the atmosphere surrounding Carey and me seemed to thicken, as if it were dense with thoughts that neither of us was speaking. After a minute she opened her knapsack and took out a pen and her notebook.

I was thinking about how much Theo's life had changed since she'd come into it, and wondering if he would snap back to his old self once we got up to Boston; assuming his parents talked him into going, which given the depth of his relationship with Carey, I wasn't at all sure was a definite. I couldn't help thinking how much simpler things were before Carey'd come into the picture. And I couldn't help resenting, a little, the way she'd kind of insinuated herself between Theo and me. About the only time we ever did anything by ourselves anymore was when we drove the ice truck. I guess I was missing the good old days. The pre-Carey days.

"You don't have to worry, Boog. I'm not going to let him not go." Carey's voice couldn't have been quieter, but it almost made me jump, the way she'd picked up on what I was thinking.

I looked over at her. She let out a slow quiet sigh and closed the notebook that lay on her lap. "I guess there's some parts of life it does no good to try and write around." She let the pen drop from her fingers to the rock, and sat there staring out into space. Real tears were rolling down her face, mixing with the bloodroot sap. Before the thought was conscious, the impulse was action; I reached over and wiped them away with my fingers.

Everything was still except for the rush of the falls.

16

THERE'S MORE THAN one kind of fog where I live. There's the kind you get when the water's warm and the air is cold; it looks like puffs of breath on a frigid winter day. There's the haze of summer that shimmers a pale bluish white and burns off by noon. Then there's the New England pea soup variety, thick coastal fog that comes from warm moist air moving in over cold water. It sets in from the Sound and sometimes moves a few miles inland, blankets the whole town, opaque, thick, and wet, the color of sooty cotton.

That's the kind that was shrouding Yardley the third Sunday in May, the day after the Yardley High senior prom. Blues Thing had played the post prom party, our last big gig. The Stones were moving even sooner than I'd thought, the first of July. It was kind of our farewell engagement, and it went well, except for the fact that Theo choked on ''Blues Stew,'' just stood there mute onstage, until I signalled the guys to go into the next number. Essentially, his body was onstage, but his spirit was off in the ozone some-where, which made for music that was polished, but soulless. Because Carey wasn't around.

In fact, she hadn't been around since that afternoon at Devil's Hollow. Theo was hurting bad.

"She won't talk to me on the phone. I've gone up a couple of times and she has the door locked and won't answer. What the hell am I supposed to do?"

I didn't know what to say to him.

Anyhow, I got up around 5:00 that afternoon, a little groggy still, after having been up all night. We hadn't finished breaking down till 4:30 A.M, then we'd gone to the diner. Mom was in the den at her com-puter, working on a series of articles about local ef-forts to clean up the Sound. Pop was snoozing on the couch. When I wandered into the kitchen in search of some sustenance, Allie was on the phone, with her hand half over her mouth, talking in hushed tones. I made myself a turkey sandwich, snagged a soda and a bag of potato chips, and was on my way back up to my room with it, when Allie hung up the phone. She scowled at me.

"What? What did I do?" I was baffled. I'd been sleeping all day.

She put her hands on her hips. "You know, you Could Call him. You've never even Asked me for his number."

I gave my head a little shake, trying to boost the necessary synapses to make this connection. "Hunh? He? You mean—Charlie?"

"No, I mean the Man in the Moon! Yes, Charlie! Remember him?"

I rolled my eyes. I was very depressed about the

band. About everything kind of coming to an end. This was the last thing I needed.

"You know, Allie, I offered to give him guitar lessons. He turned me down. Did you know that? He said he'd be too busy."

She snorted in disgust. "How Dense can you Be? He just said that so you wouldn't feel like you Had to."

Bull's-eye. I had known that. But right at that moment, I didn't feel like being forced to confront it. So I did an about-face and went back to my room.

The conversation had disturbed me enough that I was useless for any kind of creative activity or even just mundane practicing. I moseyed downstairs again, taking care to stay out of Allie's way, and went outside, thinking maybe I'd go for a drive and clear my head. But the fog was so thick, seemed like driving would require more concentration than I could drum up at that point. So I went for a walk instead.

I could hear the foghorn, a muffled bellow, like a deep slow pulse seeming to come from all directions, as if the fog diffused it. I wandered down toward the creek, trying to keep my brain as blank as the fog because everything was just too damn depressing to think about, and ended up following the inlet that goes to the boat basin as far as the Stones' backyard.

There, my feet took a turn and I wound up on the back porch. For some reason, I knocked before going in, I don't know why.

Inside, the house was in kind of a shambles, with Mrs. Stone sorting things out, getting ready to take apart eight years of her family's life. It was unsettling, to say the least. Theo's mother just gave me a little wave and pointed up to the third floor.

Up in Theo's room, things seemed more normal, the usual disarray. In the corner near his closet door was a huge packing crate, with red fragile stamps and stickers plastered all over it. He was looking out the window, in the direction of the lighthouse. Not that anything could be seen; the visibility was almost nil.

"What's that?" I asked, shoving aside a pile of books and papers on the bed to make a place to sit down.

"Hunh? Oh. Hey, Boog." He turned around and stood there, shoulders slumped. "What's what?"

I pointed at the crate. He stared at it, and gave a short, mirthless laugh.

"I guess you could call it the down payment for my new car."

"What is it?"

"It's a present for Carey," he said absently.

I was about to rephrase the question for the third time, but he swiped some sweat pants and a pile of underwear off his chair, sat, and put his hands to his head, pressing his skull so tight it looked like he was trying to keep it from splitting open.

"I don't know what to do," he said. He sounded wearier than I'd ever heard him sound.

I groped for something to say. "Theo, maybe Carey's trying to do what she thinks is best for you? Like, if you love someone, you don't want to hold them back. Maybe she's just trying to make the whole thing easier on you."

"You sound like the doctor. Do me a favor and don't say, 'If it's meant to work out, it'll work out.'

I don't buy it. Sometimes you have to make things work out.''

I decided it was time to be direct. ''Sometimes you have to know when to quit. Maybe this is the time. Maybe Carey knows it.''

We'd just finished studying Shakespeare's *Julius Caesar* in English, and the look Theo shot me then was pure ''*Et tu, Brute?*''—what Caesar said to his best friend when Brutus joined in the stabbing, murderous mob.

''You know what she says? She says when she looks in the mirror, she sees nobody. Why?'' His voice was getting louder. ''Why does she have such a lousy opinion of herself?''

''I don't know, Theo.'' It seemed like he had to talk, to get it out, so I just sat there in listening mode.

He was up and pacing. ''She's got a gift, Boog. With the writing I mean. You've seen it. I mean, she's so sensitive to everything—takes it all in and turns it into something. It's fine when it's good stuff, but she can't block out the bad stuff. It's like she gets overloaded, and then she shuts down. How do you get through to someone like that? I thought if I just loved her enough, she'd see what I see, what she's worth.''

Again, I didn't really know what to say. But he seemed to be waiting for a response of some kind now.

''I don't know if anyone can make someone else see that, you know? I think that's something we gotta do for ourselves, Theo,'' was what I finally said. ''I mean, you can help someone, or try, but the bottom line is, I think life is a pull yourself up by your own bootstrap operation. We're all on our own.''

He looked at me hard, and shook his head. "Uh-uh. I don't buy that, not the second part. Not make them maybe, but help. Don't you listen to the songs we do? You think love is just a word?"

I stayed for dinner because Mrs. Stone had cooked a huge, homemade chicken potpie and Dr. Stone had gotten an emergency call on his beeper about fifteen minutes before it was ready.

"Please stay, I made enough to feed an army. Sometimes I just can't get used to not having a full house to take care of. It feels so strange. Maybe a smaller place will be better." She sighed.

They were moving to a condo on the water, up in Marblehead, as it turned out. Mrs. Stone wanted to live near the ocean.

"I guess I must be getting old. I remember when we moved here. The change was exciting. I don't feel ready for this." She looked at Theo. "I don't feel ready for my baby to go off to college."

Theo looked tense when she said that, as if there were a slew of unspoken words he was holding in. We sat down in the breakfast room. Nobody ate much or said much either. It may have been the oppressive weight of the weather, or the weight of the near future, hovering there, but not happening yet, even though it was all decided.

"I hope this fog lifts soon," Mrs. Stone said when we finished eating. "It isn't doing anything for my spirits." She got up and started clearing the table. Her posture was kind of sagging, and for once, she looked her age, like a woman whose kids were all grown. I guess Theo saw it, too, and a spark of his old self came to the surface.

"I'll do that, Mom. You relax for a few. Here, read the paper." He picked up the as yet unread Sunday edition of the *Newbridge Post* from the hutch, set it on the table, and gently nudged her back toward her chair. "Read the funnies," he said.

She smiled at him, put an arm around his waist, and kissed him.

"Things will work out, sweetie, you'll see."

No verbal response from Theo to that remark.

I helped him clean up, while Mrs. Stone sat at the table and read the paper. I was twisting a tie around the garbage bag and Theo was scrubbing a saucepan when out of the blue, Mrs. Stone said, "Oh, dear."

"What's the matter?" Theo asked. He strolled over to the doorway between the kitchen and the breakfast room.

"Theo—" Mrs. Stone sounded very disturbed, and something else—sad maybe. I set the garbage bag down and went and stood next to Theo.

"What was the name of that older couple who lived next to Carey? Was it Benson?"

"Yeah. Why?" Theo asked.

As he asked why, it clicked in my mind, a detached observation, that Mrs. Stone had used the past tense. She held out the front section of the paper to him silently. He scanned it, then slammed it on the table.

"Shit!"

I picked it up and saw the small headline on the bottom of the front page: ELDERLY COUPLE DIES IN YARDLEY HILLS FIRE. I skimmed the column, getting goosebumps as I read.

Nathaniel and Cornelia Benson—North Road—late Saturday afternoon—house in flames by the time neighbors reported the blaze—firefighters found both bodies in the front hall about eight feet from the door—cause of fire under investigation.

I remembered that bare bulb and frayed wire in the cellar, and the rough sawn beams, and all the stuff they'd collected—a disaster waiting to happen.

Theo was whirling around the kitchen, like a cyclone looking for a point to touch down. He strode back into the breakfast room.

"Where's my jacket? Nevermind. Mom, can I borrow the car? I have to go make sure Carey's okay."

"Theo . . ." There was hesitation in Mrs. Stone's voice, like she had some grave reservation or there was something she really felt compelled to say. Theo immediately seemed to interpret it as something bad about Carey, and he wasn't about to listen.

"Forget it. Boog? You run me up?" He turned to me. I shrugged a yes kind of shrug.

"Theo." Mrs. Stone said again, and her voice was pleading now.

He stepped over to her, leaned down, and kissed her on the cheek.

"Mom, I gotta go. I love you." Then he was out the door like he'd been shot from a crossbow.

I raised an eyebrow apologetically to Mrs. Stone, hating to be in the middle. She sighed, but gave me a nod and a small tired smile.

"Drive carefully," she said.

*　　*　　*

It took us almost half an hour to get up to Carey's house.

"I can't believe she didn't call me when this happened," Theo must have said twenty times if he said it once.

The fog was as thick up in the hills as it was along the shore, and we couldn't see the main house from the road. I crawled the van up the driveway and pulled up next to the Meltzer's Nurseries pickup. There didn't seem to be any lights on inside.

Theo jumped out before I even came to a full stop, and I could hear him calling Carey as he ran toward the door. When I got out of the van, I could feel my eyes straining, the muscles in them working, but no visual input came back. It's weird how other senses take over when you can't see anything. The trees were so saturated with moisture they were dripping, and I could hear the individual drops splatter. And in the air, I could smell a faintly scorched odor, an acrid wet ash smell. When it hit me what it was, I almost gagged.

Theo was inside, switching on lights here and there as he went through the house, calling Carey's name. I wandered into the living room, then over to the door of Carey's bedroom, where Theo was standing, holding up a piece of looseleaf, reading it. I glanced around the room and blinked. On top of a layer of basic mess, like Allie's room, it was strewn with dozens of hats. It looked like the Mad Hatter had been there and gone completely bonkers. A bunch of empty wine cooler bottles were on the floor.

The expression on Theo's face was an odd one of despair mixed with a glimmer of hope. He handed the paper to me. Lyrics called, "Hope in Your Eyes," sloppily written, but not worked and reworked, with no punctuation, as if the words had just come streaming out.

> There are nights like a cave
> So dark and black
> They swallow me whole
> There are nights like a rack
> Stretched out so taut
> I feel I'm breaking
> Can't tell the nightmares
> From the waking
>
> There are days like a chasm
> I stand on the edge
> Try to keep my balance
> There are days like a hedge
> So thick with thorns
> I can't get through
> Without being pierced
> So what do I do
>
> I listen and all I hear is fear
> Howling like a demon in my ear
> I'm afraid to live—afraid to die
> I'm afraid it's all a lie
> Living's really dying in disguise
> I see my only hope in your eyes
>
> There are times like an ocean
> Wave after wave
> of sorrow to drown in
> What can save

That was it. She hadn't finished the last verse. I read it through a second time while Theo just stood there, because something about it made my mind go askew. Then I realized it was the way she'd sprung the sense of the lines around the rhyme scheme, from the first part of the verse to the second—with the right music it would work.

"Where the hell do you suppose she is?" Theo said.

"She's gone." The raspy voice behind us made us both jump. Mr. Harrigan was sagging against the door frame, looking like he'd crawled out of a shallow grave, his skin gray, unshaven, his chin trembling, his eyes bleary and bloodshot. I had to take a step back to avoid inhaling the fumes. He must have been sweating ninety proof. Theo took one look at him and bounded over, grabbing him by the front of his shirt.

"What do you mean, gone? Where?"

Carey's dad cringed a little in the face of Theo's rage. He gave a weak effort at a shrug.

"Gone," he whispered. "Said there's nothing for her here."

"When did she leave? Where was she going? Is she walking? What? What? Tell me you son of a—" I'd never seen Theo lose it like this.

All of a sudden, Mr. Harrigan began to sob, and at that, Theo's anger seemed to drain or at least get under control. He took a deep breath, let it out slowly, and let go of the shirt.

"Come on, Boog." He shouldered past Carey's father, and I went with him.

In the van, I turned the key, and sat there idling, looking at Theo.

"Any idea where she might have headed?" I asked.

"I don't know. She took all her notebooks with her though. They weren't on the little book rack on her desk. I can't imagine where..." He chewed his thumbnail, frowning. "Maybe if we drive around—if she's walking—if she didn't leave that long ago. I don't know...." He sounded tired and confused.

I thought of that unfinished verse she'd left behind, then of her mother and the word drowning, and a shiver struck me. An instinct.

"Why don't we head up toward Devil's Hollow," I suggested, keeping my voice casual.

He nodded. "Okay."

We overtook her on the hairpin turn just before the access road, a lumpy gray shadow, weaving a little unsteadily on the side of the road.

I pulled ahead of her a little, then swung the van over, blocking her way. Theo got out and led her over. She didn't protest, didn't say anything at all as he took her stuff, a duffel bag and her knapsack, tossed it in back, and helped her up into the front seat with him. She had on a little-old-lady type hat, and I wondered if Mrs. Benson had given it to her.

"Where were you going?" he asked gently.

"I don't know," she whispered. "Away. Somewhere else." Her voice sounded slurry, and she punctuated her sentence with a hiccup.

Theo wrapped his arms around her, and let out a slow sigh. "How about we go for some coffee?"

She hiccuped again. " 'Kay."

He looked at me.

"I'm just the driver," I said. "Whatever you want to do."

"Sunday night—closest place open is probably the pit stop on the parkway."

I nodded, eased the van along the shoulder to the access road where I could swing a *U*, then headed south toward the entrance ramp. As we drove, he talked to her softly.

"I'm sorry about Mr. and Mrs. Benson, baby. I'm sorry about your old man. I'm sorry so many things in your life are so lousy right now. But running away's not going to do any good."

Her head kind of rolled, slumping down against his shoulder, and she didn't answer. I slipped a cassette into the deck, B. B. King, "Indianola Mississippi Seeds."

The parkway was pretty empty. It's not the preferred road in bad weather, being unlit and hilly, with narrow lanes; I kept the speedometer hovering around forty-eight mph. Ten minutes later, we were chugging up the long steep rise, then pulling into the dimly lit service area. I felt the need to stretch my legs.

"I'll go. You want one, too, Theo?" I said, fishing around in the ashtray for change.

"Yeah. Thanks. I have a feeling it's gonna be a long night," Theo said.

"No. Not coffee." Carey was alive again. "Hot cocoa."

"Car, you really should have coffee," Theo cajoled her.

"No!" Her voice got louder, and stubborn, like a little kid's. "Hot cocoa. I want hot cocoa like Mrs. Benson makes. Mrs. Benson—" Her voice, still slurry, broke a little.

"Okay, okay," Theo said. "Hot cocoa, I guess, Boog. It's got some caffeine in it."

"Fine." I got out with my handful of change.

Sorry as I felt for Carey at that moment, I was losing patience with her act, and wished she'd wise up and get it together.

I went up to the vending machine that dispensed coffee, tea, cocoa, and chicken bouillon, pouring it down spouts into Styrofoam cups, and slid in some coins, then punched the button for cocoa. I groaned as the EMPTY PLEASE MAKE ANOTHER SELECTION sign lit up. Swearing under my breath, I got three coffees, thinking it was probably better this way: cocoa on top of wine coolers was liable to make Carey puke all over the van. Plus, I figured in her current state, she probably wouldn't be able to tell the difference between it and a light and sweet coffee anyhow.

I figured wrong. She took one sip, held the cup out the window that Theo'd opened to get her some fresh air, and dumped it.

"I want cocoa," she insisted.

"The machine was out of cocoa," I said tersely.

"Aw, Carey, come on." Even Theo's patience was wearing thin, I could tell. "All right, the other side might have it. Stay here. I'll be right back."

He handed me his cup to hold, and opened the door, propped Carey up, and closed it. Then he headed in the direction of the road, disappearing in the fog halfway to the median.

Carey reached over to turn up the volume on the tape. I snapped it off. She slouched back in the seat. I could feel irritation growing in me, so I didn't say anything or look at her, just looked out the window, waiting for Theo to get back with the damn cocoa. I heard the door in the reststop building across the parkway close, and the faint padding of rapid footsteps. At the same time, I heard the Doppler drone of a car on the northbound side, our side. It all converged in a hazy burst of diffused light—high beams and fog lamps coming up and over the top of the hill—a loud but muffled thud—no horn—no yell—a shrieking, twisted skid—the metallic rasp of a car scraping the divider, of steel sheering, crumpling—that was it.

Two ambulances. One for Theo, who was killed instantly, and one for the poor slob who'd just been driving along, not even speeding, minding his own business, who never even saw him because of the fog. The questions almost did me in. Who were we, who was he, why had he been crossing the parkway. I was numb, but they just kept asking and asking in quiet, concerned, but stern voices. I didn't even see the faces after a while. I don't know what they did with Carey, brought her home I assumed, like they did with me, because my hands were shaking too hard to hold the wheel. Pop went up and got the van the next day.

The only thing I remember about the next night, while they were still making the arrangements, was Hum howling like he was gonna howl his throat right out. That and everyone tiptoeing around me.

There's a sound that's not a sound in the same room as a dead person, the sound of one person not breathing, almost the sound of one heart not beating. It's very noticeable. There's nothing stiller than a coffin. Theo's was closed. In front of this huge blanket of gold roses was his senior picture. Dr. and Mrs. Stone had asked me if I wanted to see him with the family in private. View the remains, the undertaker called it. I didn't. I didn't want a picture of Theo's body without him in it engraved in my brain.

"Are you sure?" Mom asked me. "Sometimes it helps to say good-bye."

Nothing was going to help this. And I didn't want to say good-bye. I wanted to say, "Hey, Theo, come on, don't be a slacker. Get up. We have things to do."

The wake ran two nights. I went for both of them. I remembered when my grandfather died at eighty-two, it was almost like a family party. Catching up on news of cousins and people we hadn't seen in a while, reminiscing about what a good long life he'd had, even laughing quietly here and there. There was a sense of relief because he'd been pretty sick and his suffering was over.

Theo's wake was different. The whole scenario reeked of reality gone wrong, of something that wasn't supposed to be happening. The funeral home was crammed with people. Family. Aunts, uncles. Zillions of friends of all the family members. People from Theo's church. Dr. Stone's colleagues. Teachers. Kids from school and their parents. Dr. and Mrs. Stone and the rest of Theo's immediate family stood in a line on the far side of the coffin. The line of people waiting to go through and express their condolences was out the front door most of the time. Some people hugged the family, some shook hands, some people wept, and a few times, I saw tears slide down from behind the tinted glasses Mrs. Stone was wearing.

The first thing you do is sign the sympathy book. You walk by all the flowers, and look at them while you wait your turn to go and kneel on the kneeler in front of the coffin. Mom and Allie went first. Allie was clinging to Mom like a little kid, looking petrified. I went next, by myself. I knelt down and tried to think of a prayer or something. Nothing came to mind. I noticed the grain in the wood of the coffin, beneath the shiny varnish. Not a single fingerprint on it; unthinkable to touch it.

I looked at Theo's picture and couldn't connect with it. It was like it was some kid I didn't know. Then it came over me suddenly, the realization that it was Theo inside that box and at the same time, this crazy impulse to yank it open, grab him, and just get him the hell out of there. Pop came up behind me, put a hand on my shoulder, and we went over to the Stones.

Mrs. Stone hugged me for a long moment. She looked like she was trying to say something, but she couldn't. I couldn't speak either. I wondered if she blamed me in some way for giving Theo a ride when she'd had obvious misgivings. We nodded at each other a few times, and I moved down the line. Then we went and sat in one of the rows of chairs set out for the mourners.

The second night when I knelt on the kneeler, all I could think about was that I heard Mrs. Stone say they had to bury Theo in one of Eric's suits, because he hadn't worn one in so long, he didn't have one that fit. That seemed wrong to me, like, something unofficial about it, like they were burying the wrong person, because Theo wouldn't be caught dead in a suit.

When that thought passed through my mind, I almost lost it and laughed out loud because there he was, dead in a suit, a few inches of wood away from me. I put my head in my hands so no one would see and tried to pray again. Nothing.

That second night, Natalie Stewart was there with her folks, and from the way she was weeping, you would have thought she and Theo had been engaged. She was big-time into letting people comfort her, which really rubbed me the wrong way. I tried to steer clear of her.

I was out in the lobby with Danny, Peter, and Keith, who came together. I was starting to get the hang of the wake thing. You go in, mourn, condole, then go out for a breather, then go back in for as long as you can stand it, the weight of all that grief, then take five again, and so on until it's over. You just wait for it to be over. You don't think about what comes next because it's like time is stopped dead in its tracks.

I was standing by the sympathy book podium, with the guys, when I felt a sharp poke in the ribs.

"Look at her," Natalie hissed in my ear.

I looked over toward the doorway and saw Carey step unsteadily inside. Our eyes met and she made a move toward me. She was a wreck. Her hair was limp, her face blotchy. Her outfit was some bedraggled combination totally inappropriate for the occasion, even making an exception for her personal style. And she was wearing a green Robin Hood type hat with a long feather in it. And the Headhunter's joke popped into my mind, and I heard Theo laughing, Theo's voice saying, "Oh no, not another hat!" Something in me got ready to go nuts.

She opened her mouth, and I could smell the alcohol on her breath.

"I'm sorry. . . ." she whispered.

All I could think of was what it would do to Theo's parents if they had to deal with this. I grabbed her sleeve and pulled her out the front door and into the parking lot.

"You're sorry? You're sorry?" I started in a whisper, but I couldn't contain the fury that was building up inside me. "I'll say you're sorry. You're about the sorriest excuse for a human being I've ever seen. Sorry? What good does that do?" My voice was getting louder and out of the corner of my eyes, I saw Keith running down the steps with Miss Brockmeyer and another teacher who'd been in the lobby. "Carey Question Mark Harrigan. You know what your middle name is? Pathetic. Disaster. Your middle name is Death!" I shouted. "Theo'd be alive if it wasn't for you."

I let go of her arm and she sagged, like she was going to fall down right there in the parking lot. Miss Brockmeyer stepped around us and caught her. Keith was next to me, trying to grab onto me.

"Boog, take it easy, man," he was saying.

I shouldered him out of the way and started walking toward the exit. When I got to the road, I broke into a run. I ripped off my jacket and my tie, threw them down, then just kept running.

chapter 17

*A BELL RINGING —an old black-and-white movie—
with a happy ending—angel gets his wings—rings
again—the dream I'm half-aware is a dream changes
scenes—the bell buoy that marks the entrance to the
channel—wings stretched out against a clear blue
sky—a seagull gliding on a thermal just offshore—
I'm in the middle of the channel, treading water,
while the current of the outgoing tide sweeps by without carrying me along with it, flowing around me—
way out, halfway to the lighthouse, I can see a raft,
with a person on it—I know it's Theo and I'm trying
to will him to turn around and at least wave, but he
doesn't—bell rings a third time—my mind pops into
conscious mode.*

In the space of a minute, a memory reel clicks on and
replays the first day we met:

I followed him out behind the old Captain Lemual
B. Goodman house, down the sloping back yard to

203

the creek. There was a pile of old boards and debris, from some renovations being done on the house.

"Look at all this stuff!" He spread his arms out and grinned.

"Looks like trash to me," I said.

"Look again," he said, grinning. "We got everything we need to make a raft. If we hurry, we can catch the tide out to the lighthouse."

We didn't catch the tide that day. In fact, it took us most of the summer to put together something that didn't sink like a box of rocks the second we got on it. Theo never got discouraged, though. "Hey, so what?" he'd say after each unsuccessful launch. "So we try again." He seemed to get as much enjoyment out of the process, maybe more, as he did out of the final product itself.

Middle of August though, we finally managed to float one. We launched it from Theo's backyard, and left Hum barking on the shore. It rode a little low in the water, but it didn't get swamped. The tide caught us, and we started to drift out the channel. And I remember feeling like I was really going someplace— I didn't know where, but it was someplace new—and the freedom of that feeling nearly ripped my chest open.

We drifted out as far as the bell buoy before the local marine police pulled us over and made us climb into the cutter. We were drenched, so they threw some blankets around our shoulders, then lectured us on not having personal flotation devices, operating an unsafe vessel, *yada yada yada*. They towed the raft in and impounded it, then escorted us home to our respective parents. But it didn't even matter by then. Theo and

I had gone someplace, someplace right there, but at the same time, a world away, and there was no back-tracking.

The way the sun's slanting through my window, I know it's midafternoon. I don't remember falling asleep, but I guess I finally drifted off. The memory of the dream itself is fading, but the feeling of it is staying with me.

I lie there, thinking if I get up and go look out the window, what I'll see is the Goodman house. It's empty again, has been since the Stones moved, back in July. Empty. That's how I've been feeling for too long. I'm remembering how Hum howled every night for two weeks after Theo died, so loud I could hear him with my window closed. Theo's blues hound. The way he sounded was the way I felt.

Some serious pounding on my door makes me jump. Not Mom, or Pop, they're more subtle in their attempts to lure me out of my room for the inevitable chats on how life has to go on, and Theo wouldn't want to see me this way. Anyhow, they're both at work.

"Damn it, James, open this door or—"

It's Allie. There's a frantic edge to her tone that puts me on alert. I drag myself up, pull on a shirt, and I'm dressed, having slept in my blue jeans. I pad over to the door, twist the knob, and unlock it. She's on me like a piranha, her jaw in overdrive.

"Hurry up, we have to go. Where are your shoes? Would you Please hurry, God, I never saw anyone so slow." She's down on the floor on her hands and knees, hunting through the debris for my shoes. She finds them under a pizza carton and chucks them at me.

"Allie, what is it?" I step into my shoes without untying the laces and work them over my heels.

"Somebody just called. We have to go to Newbridge Hospital. It's Charlie."

The panic in her voice jolts me. I realize it's been months since I gave Charlie a thought—Charlie or anyone or anything really. I wasn't even aware Allie was still in touch with him. Something in me opens up and then almost as suddenly, gets ready to shut right back down.

No, I think. Uh-uh. Count me out.

"Who called?" I hear myself ask.

She's tugging me out the door. "I don't know. A woman—I forget her name."

"What did she say?"

Allie's got my keys in her hand, and she's behind me now, pushing me out the door.

"She said, 'Tell James to come to Newbridge Hospital emergency room. Tell him Charlie needs him.' "

I stop thinking and just go. We're at the hospital in less than fifteen minutes. We park, and then we're both out and running, through the automatic glass doors, into the lobby.

The hospital has its own set of sounds and smells. It smells of disinfectant and metal and clean sheets. The sounds are equipment beeps, distant phones ringing, and the rapid squeaking of rubber-soled shoes. It's quiet and urgent.

I spot Mac Winters talking to the nurse behind the reception desk just outside the ER. He doesn't see me. I walk over and touch his sleeve.

"Mac."

He frowns as he looks up, then the frown turns into recognition as he places me.

"James!"

"Is Charlie all right? What happened?"

"Wait just a minute, okay?" He has another word with the nurse, then walks over to the waiting area across the hall, gesturing me and Allie to follow. We all sit down in the tweed-covered chairs. Mac smiles at my sister.

"You must be Allie. Charlie mentioned you. Several times, in fact."

"Allie, this is Mac Winters, from Anchor House."

Allie nods. "What happened to Charlie, Mr. Winters?"

Mac presses his fingertips together and sighs, but he doesn't duck the question.

"His mother's boyfriend went on a rampage again. Charlie put himself in the line of fire."

For some reason, the old saying, "Fools rush in where angels fear to tread," passes through my mind. And I'm seeing Charlie's face, only it's superimposed by Theo's, they're blurred together, and I'm thinking, I bet Theo'll show those angels a thing or two about treading in. Theodore Haley Stone. Hero. Then I have to close my eyes, because they're stinging so bad.

"I don't know how the social worker missed it, his being back in the picture, but the caseloads are so heavy and things slip through the cracks sometimes. And Charlie didn't tell anyone, I guess he didn't want to see the family split up again."

I open my eyes and look Mac square in his. "How bad is it?"

"He'll live," Mac says. His voice has a hard edge to it, but his eyes belie his tone. "A broken wrist, a dislocated shoulder, a mild concussion. The boyfriend's in jail."

A woman's voice interrupts—a familiar one. One I listened to all last year.

"Mac, I'm going to head back over to Anchor House now."

I turn around, and Miss Brockmeyer smiles at me, pats my arm, then heads for the exit.

I stare at her, with the feeling that there's something I want to ask her, but I can't figure out what it is. The picture of her and Carey in the parking lot outside of the funeral home flashes through my mind. That was the last time I saw Carey; she never came back to school. And I'm remembering what I said to her, and something in me is recoiling at the memory of myself, that I could have said something that could hurt so much. I push it out of my mind.

"Can we see Charlie now?" Allie's asking.

Mac nods. "I think so. Let me go check."

He's gone and then he's back, beckoning us over to the emergency room treatment area. We follow him down to the third cubicle, step around the long beige partition curtain. And there he is. He's got a black eye and one hand has an IV needle taped to it, and the other one's encased in white plaster from the knuckles to the elbow. His mouth stretches into a weak grin when he sees us.

"Hey, Buglioni. Hi, Allie, you're looking good."

"And you're looking terrible," Allie says. I can see she's horrified, and close to tears, which always makes her a little pugnacious. She walks over to the bed, leans down, and kisses him on the cheek. Charlie looks embarrassed, but he grins.

"I guess you won't be able to play the guitar for a while," I say. "But how about starting up with lessons again when you get that thing off?"

A frown settles on his forehead, like the shadow of a cloud on an otherwise sunny beach.

"What?" I say.

"That bastard." He says it through gritted teeth.

"What's the matter, Charlie?" Mac asks.

Charlie swallows and looks away from us, glances back for a moment at me, then looks away again.

Mac motions Allie to go with him and leave us alone. I move up closer to the head of the bed, pull over the molded plastic chair, and sit.

"Tell me about it, Charlie."

"I was playing—you know, I think I got part of that 'Boogie Man' song down, I'm not sure, I couldn't remember how you did it, but—" His voice is choking up a little.

"Yeah? And?" I prod, gently.

"He broke it. I came down when he started yelling and I had it in my hand and he grabbed it and—" His face is tight, but I can see in his eyes that the broken guitar hurts worse than the broken wrist. And I feel sick as I picture the scene. Charlie sniffs and tries to wipe his eyes, but one hand's hooked to the tube and the other's in the cast. There's a box of Kleenex on the table next to me. I snatch a wad and blot the leakage for him. I take a deep breath and exhale slowly.

"It's okay, Charlie. It's a piece of wood. A nice piece of wood," I can't help saying, just in honor of the Guild. "But it's a thing. We can get it fixed. Or find another one."

What I'm saying isn't enough. I put my hand on his shoulder and feel the tension through the flimsy hospital gown.

"Charlie, remember that day you came over my house, took the bus?"

He nods.

"We were working on a song before you got there, our first original. Carey and Theo wrote it. The last line goes, 'The magic's in you.' It's like that with music. He can't touch that, or break it, or take it away from you. No one can. Okay? Got it?"

After a few seconds, he nods again.

"Yeah," he says, his voice a little croaky. "Got it."

I stand up casually, to give him some space to collect himself.

"I'll go get Allie. She can play doctor."

Now the cocky grin is back. "You trust me playing doctor alone with your sister?"

"As long as both your hands are tied up like that," I say and grin back.

Mac's on the phone out in the hall, and Allie's sitting back in the waiting area. She jumps up and comes running over to me.

"Your turn," I say.

She's off like a shot before I have a chance to add any words of Big Brotherly advice.

Mac and I chat for a few minutes.

"So what's going to happen with Charlie?" I ask. "Is he going back with his mother, even though the guy's in jail? How can you make sure something like this doesn't happen again?''

Mac passes a hand over his hair wearily. "I don't know yet, James. We don't have an opening at Anchor House at the moment. We'll probably try to find at least a temporary foster situation. There are limits to our resources and our mandate." He sighs, and I know exactly how he feels; like he failed when it counted most. And I realize that behind blaming Carey, I've been blaming myself for somehow not stopping what happened to Theo from happening.

This strange feeling comes over me, this surge of half recklessness, half courage, maybe. And I'm seeing Theo on top of Devil's Ledge, and then it's me up there: In my mind, my arms are stretched out, ready to go for it, head first, dive into deep clean water.

"Let me talk to my parents, Mac. We have an extra bedroom." I say the words, then I wait for my sensible self to start in babbling all the reasons why having Charlie live with us would not be a good idea. Total silence.

Allie and I don't talk on the way back to Yardley. She goes straight to her room when we get home, lost in her own thoughts. And I'm swimming in mine, all murky, like the creek on a choppy day when the sediment's stirred up. I go in the kitchen, feeling ravenous all of a sudden, hungrier than I've felt in months, and see the mail on the kitchen counter, two letters to me that stop me cold. One's a small envelope postmarked Marblehead, with the Stones' return address engraved on it; the other's postmarked New

Hope, Pennsylvania, and I'd recognize the handwriting anywhere. Carey's.

It shakes me up way inside, remembering last night when I couldn't sleep, when I was waiting for some kind of sign. I'm wondering if this is it. But it's not clarifying anything. What I need is a billboard with it all spelled out, in plain block letters.

My hand drops to Carey's letter first, and I open it, feeling very strange, kind of outside myself, and start reading.

Dear Boog,

So much I've wanted to say to you, but I'm not sure any of it will come out right. I'm not even sure you won't rip up this letter. I wouldn't blame you if you did. Remember that first day in Brockmeyer's class, when she asked how I personally could make the world a better place and I said something like, "Move to another planet?" Well, that's what I wanted to do after that night—only one thing stopped me—it would turn everything Theo gave to me, everything he did for me into a waste. Scum-of-the-earth lowlife as I seem to myself sometimes, I can't do that. I can't do it to him.

Speaking of Brockmeyer, if you ever see her tell her I say hi and thanks, okay? And that I'm taking a few courses, trying to make up what I missed, and have a part-time job at a florist. She asked me to write and let her know, but it's really hard for me to write anything these days, so I haven't. Her bringing me back to Anchor

House the night of the wake was kind of a turning point for my father, I think. She and Mac did a lot to help us get these arrangements worked out—we're in Pennsylvania, living with my aunt and uncle. Ironic to come to a place called New Hope, but, things are, well, a little better. He's been going to AA, part of the deal with his brother.

Anyway, last night I was coming home from work, and Stevie Ray's "Life Without You" came on the radio. I knew there was only one person who would know how it made me feel, and that's you. It seemed like kind of a sign that I should get in touch with you.

If you don't write back, I'll understand, but here's the address in case you ever decide to.

—Carey

A sign, she wrote. I stare at the letter, then I'm not seeing it anymore, I'm listening to Stevie Ray singing and playing in my head, as sweet and mournful a slow blues as you ever wanna hear.

Well hello baby, tell me how have you been?
We all have missed you and the way you grin.
But the day is necessary ev'ry now and then.
For souls to move on givin' life back again.

Fly on fly on, fly on my friend,
Go on, live again love again.

Day after day, night after night,
Second guessing ev'ry ev'ry minute as the years go
*   passing by. Bye, bye, bye.*
Alarmed if in the mirror we come face to face.

Wishing all the love, love we took for granted
  Lord we had today.

Life without you all the love you passed our way.
The angels have waited for so long now they have
  their way. Take your place.

I let the whole guitar solo play out in my mind, and my fingers are aching to play along with it, the first time I've felt that since Theo died. And I'm thinking about why I love the blues so much. It's music that gets right at the heart of life, even the part that hurts, even death.

I put Carey's letter down, wondering if I will write back, and pick up the other letter, the third one I've gotten from Theo's mom, and a drop splashes on the envelope, blurring the zip code, then another. Shit. I take a deep breath and open it.

Dear Boog,

I'm sorry I haven't written in a while. There are days when I find myself having to overcome a terrible inertia just to get out of bed in the morning. But they are getting fewer and farther between. I was finally able to bring myself to go through Theo's things, which as you know, I had the movers pack up when we left Yardley. Which brings me to the point of this note. I'll be sending some things to you that I think he'd want you to have. But there's an item here, a Celtic harp, which he had planned to give to Carey when we moved. The doctor almost went through the roof when Theo told him what he'd bought instead of putting the money down on a new car. But he agrees with me that we should send it to Carey because that's what Theo would want. So if you could send me a current address for her, I'd be very grateful.

Meanwhile, I know you've postponed your plans for music school—don't postpone life too long, dear. If anything, think of Theo and live it twice as fully.

Much love,
Ingrid Stone

A harp. Theo bought a harp instead of a car. I feel a chuckle rising inside me, and shake my head. Theo to a *T*: see two ways to go, and go for the one that takes more heart. A harp.

I put Mrs. Stone's letter back on the counter, and let out a long slow exhale. And I'm thinking, life— it's so damn risky. And love. As soon as you risk loving someone, you risk losing them. And I'm thinking about how some people have such a hard time loving, and maybe fear of that loss is the reason, but others, a special few, like Theo, are born geniuses at it.

His voice is back, but it's different than it's been, more like I know it's inside my head, more the quality of a daydream than a hallucination. And there's mischief in it, like he's grinning.

How's that for a sign, Boog? Clear enough?

I chuckle and wipe my eyes on my sleeve.

"Clear as a bell, Theo. . . ."